PENGUIN METRO READS

PAPERBACK DREAMS

Rahul Saini is the bestselling author of three hugely popular novels *Those Small Lil Things*, *Just Like in the Movies* and *The Orange Hangover*. Formerly an architect, he has a keen interest in photography, film-making and fine arts. Currently he serves as a visiting faculty member for an art and design program at a prestigious university in India. He takes an active interest in the wellness of his students.

From the small Punjabi town of Jalandhar, he is a high-spirited young man who spends much of his time travelling, mostly to parts of Himachal Pradesh. He loves spending time with his family and friends.

PAPERBACK DREAMS

RAHUL SAINI

Penguin
metro reads

PENGUIN METRO READS

Published by the Penguin Group

Penguin Books India Pvt. Ltd, 11 Community Centre, Panchsheel Park, New Delhi 110 017, India

Penguin Group (USA) Inc., 375 Hudson Street, New York, New York 10014, USA

Penguin Group (Canada), 90 Eglinton Avenue East, Suite 700, Toronto, Ontario, M4P 2Y3, Canada (a division of Pearson Penguin Canada Inc.)

Penguin Books Ltd, 80 Strand, London WC2R 0RL, England

Penguin Ireland, 25 St Stephen's Green, Dublin 2, Ireland (a division of Penguin Books Ltd)

Penguin Group (Australia), 707 Collins Street, Melbourne, Victoria 3008, Australia (a division of Pearson Australia Group Pty Ltd)

Penguin Group (NZ), 67 Apollo Drive, Rosedale, Auckland 0632, New Zealand (a division of Pearson New Zealand Ltd)

Penguin Books (South Africa) (Pty) Ltd, Block D, Rosebank Office Park, 181 Jan Smuts Avenue, Parktown North, Johannesburg 2193, South Africa

Penguin Books Ltd, Registered Offices: 80 Strand, London WC2R 0RL, England

First published in Penguin Metro Reads by Penguin Books India 2013

10 9 8 7 6 5 4 3 2 1

ISBN 9780143421412

Typeset in Adobe Garamond by R. Ajith Kumar, New Delhi
Printed at Manipal Technologies Ltd, Manipal

For the monkey, who teaches us how to jump.

Here's to you free souls, you firefly chasers,
Tree climbers, porch swingers, air guitar players,
Here's to you fearless dancers, shaking walls in your bedrooms.

There's a lot of wonder left inside of me and you,
Thank God even crazy dreams come true.

—Carrie Underwood,
Smash, 'Callbacks' (S01E02)

When love beckons you, follow him,
Though his ways are hard and steep.

—*The Prophet*,
Khalil Gibran

1

One hot summer afternoon, when reality pinches him in a busy market street at Connaught Place, New Delhi—Rohit

This is not how it is supposed to be. I am an author. I am supposed to be rich, have a huge mansion for a house somewhere in the mountains, drive around in a luxury sedan and have a playful golden retriever named Friend. My life should be glamorous and most of all I should not have to think twice before buying the new boxed set of the hardback editions of *A Song of Ice and Fire*.

I am at the Universal Book Store in CP, holding this luxury boxed set in my hands. The books inside have that golden paint on the edges of the pages and the whole effect is hypnotic. I *need* to buy this! I turn the heavy box around and look at the price tag and get a jolt. It costs ten freaking grand! Without another thought I put the lovely box back on the shelf and start to walk away. I run my eyes through the books on the shelf and see two copies of my own book meekly stacked

towards the end. I pick up one and open it. The first thing I
see is a hideous picture of myself beaming back at me goofily.
I look like a monkey. No, truly! Why did I even decide to put
my picture in the book? I am sure it has affected sales by at
least 40 per cent. I leaf through the pages and remember why
I came to the store in the first place—I needed to investigate
the sale figures for my book. And I can't simply march to the
cash counter and demand the details. I know all shopkeepers
hate that. So I take the book over to the counter, ask the man
behind to bill it and casually say, 'How is this book doing by
the way?'

~

'Who does that? I mean … *who does that*?' My thoughts are
almost jammed as I can't think of words to express myself.

'Would you just calm down, Rohit? Just take a deep
breath … '

'Take a deep breath? *Take a deep breath!* My publisher is
cheating me. He has swindled me out of more than 40 lakh
rupees and you are asking me to take a deep breath? God!' I
cut Nisha off mid-sentence as I yell into the phone.

'You are a national bestselling author, Rohit. This behaviour
does not suit you.'

I take a deep breath and look around me—there are actually
some people who have stopped moving and are gaping at me.
One of them looks as frozen as the ice cream she is holding
in her hand. It is a marketplace. I must control myself. I have
been roaming around the crowded colonnade of CP for over

three hours now on this hot summer afternoon, hopping from one bookstore to another. I have been suspicious about the royalty figure my publisher has been giving me for the past two years and today I decided to come and do a sort of market survey myself to check the sale figures of my books. Having written a book that frequently appears in various bestsellers' lists, I believe I should get a decent royalty at the end of each year. But I don't.

'How do you know for sure he is cheating you? What proof do you have?' Nisha asks, sighing tiredly.

I hate it when she does that! She always takes the other person's side. I have known her since college. She is smart and usually gives good, rational and unbiased advice.

'What do you mean, how am I sure? I have visited twenty-three bookstores in the past three days. I took the monthly sale figures from each of them for my books, added them up, multiplied the sum by twelve and arrived at a figure that was one-third the total royalty my publisher has given me. My book sells nationally. Now, if one market is selling these many books, imagine what the total amount would be. God! I feel like … infesting his whole office and warehouse with mice. That would destroy all the stock and the black money he has stored there!'

'Don't be foolish! How do you know that he stores all his black money in his office?'

'Damn it!'

Silence

'What should I do?' I ask

'File a law suit against him,' she says easily.

'I can't do that, I have no proof.'

The words come out almost as an honest reflex and I can see her smiling at the end of the line.

'Try threatening him. Try telling him that you have found out how he has been cheating you and that you will file a case against him if he does not pay you properly.'

I don't know why she always does that. I don't know why she asks me to do things that I am incapable of doing. I am not a … a threatening kind of a person. If she told me to run into his office, scream for a few good seconds about how I know he isn't giving me the money he owes me and then frantically run out … I could do that. But that's not what she is suggesting. Moreover, that would only make him more sure and confident about the idea that he can pay me even less than what he is paying right now.

'Write a mail then,' she says.

'Hmm, yes, a mail might do, I think.'

There is silence for a moment and I can sense something coming from her.

'I don't know why you don't understand that you cannot earn a living from your writing,' she finally speaks up.

And I don't know why she is so negative at times. We have had this discussion (argument rather) so many times in the past and I am just not in the mood for it right now.

'It's not a question of earning a living out of my writing but getting what is rightfully mine,' I say.

'The question is also when are you going to end this sabbatical you are on and start thinking maturely about responsibilities like supporting yourself financially for example.'

Silence.

She is right. It has been over four months since I quit my last job hoping that the royalties from my books would be enough to support me. (And also because my boss was the most disturbingly wicked person ever, which was actually the main reason why I left.)

'I need to take up a job. Maybe I can take up a job for what I like doing second best—teaching.'

2

Flying high in the sky, on his way back from Bangalore, he is living his dream—Jeet

The airhostess looks beautiful and has the most beautiful voice too. I can't take my eyes off her as she makes the announcement that the flight is ready for takeoff. I buckle my seatbelt and take a deep breath. Another city covered, another event done—only six more to go for this year now.

It has been over nineteen months since my debut novel was released but it feels like only yesterday that I signed the contract with my publisher. The plane is in the air now and gaining altitude. I pull out the magazine section of the *Indian Times* from the sleeve below the foldable tray in front of me where I had kept it. They have done a good job again—they have given full-page coverage to my event at the Red Bookstore, Bangalore. They're carrying a big picture of me with my killer smile and there's surprisingly not even one negative thing about me this time. It's the truth, dude—paying the PR pays. Besides, how could they have written anything bad about me? The event was a huge success. All the people working at the store acknowledged that it was the biggest crowd that any event had pulled in in the last three years. They didn't even have enough chairs to accommodate the crowd. So many of them were standing there, only to see me and to listen to what I had to say. God, it felt great. After reading the article once again from beginning to end, I fold the paper and put it back in the sleeve. All this is good but how long will it go on? How the hell am I going to get another novel out with my name as the author? Getting my first book published and becoming this phenomenal success is a miracle. I may or may not deserve all this success and all this recognition, but it is mine for now and I have to find a way to retain it. *I have to find a way*.

I look outside and I see the people, the roads, the houses, the trees, all shrinking in size as we climb higher. The whole world looks like a toy game, easy to play with. Soon we reach cloud level and the view is lost. I turn my head to see if there are any beautiful chicks inside the plane. I spot a cute girl sitting in the aisle seat one row ahead of me on the opposite side. She is looking directly at me. I stare back at her and our eyes meet.

Okay, man! This is no unintentional, casual look she is giving me. She is throwing a clear line and I've got to respond. I nod my head in my signature 'What's up?' gesture and shoot my killer smile. She smiles back. Okay, life is set! I have had this fantasy for a long time now, the most common one—to have crazy, animal sex in the airplane lavatory and I have a very strong feeling that it's gonna come true today. It's a two and a half hour journey and I have enough time to just do it! This plane is gonna take off, man! Fifteen minutes from now, I am going to get up, walk to the toilet and 'accidently' brush her shoulder, apologize for the 'unintended' incident, strike up a conversation, throw in a few 'fictional facts' and that's it! The rest will be history. Just fifteen minutes, during which I am going to listen to music on my iPod and not look at her even once.

I am through one song (three and a half minutes long) when I sense movement. This is amazing, dude! The hot chick has just got up and is coming towards me with her eyes fixed on me.

'Hi,' she says, standing by me in the aisle.

'Hello,' I put in casually.

'You look familiar.'

'Is it?' I say as I flash a half smile.

'Are you Jeet Obiroi?'

'Yes,' I say, looking back at her intently.

'Oh my god, oh my god, *oh my god*!' she freaks out, 'I am your biggest fan ever!'

'Thank you,' I smile.

'Your book … *If I Would Not Have Met U … I Would Have Died* is the best book ever! I read it in two days straight!'

I smile again. She is a reader. Easy.

'Can I please take a picture with you? Please, please, *please*?'

'Sure.' Why on earth would I ever say no?

She looks at the guy sitting next to me and says, 'Sir, can I please sit in your seat for a while?'

He makes an awkward face.

'Please, sir, please, please, *please*! Only for … ten seconds, *please*!'

He gets up without saying anything and shoots me an angry look.

'Thank you! You are my god from now on! You are the *best*,' she says to the man and takes his seat while the man stands in the aisle with a blank expression on his face.

'Can you please click a picture for us?' she asks, offering her smartphone to the man. He stands there looking at her, expressionless.

'You just have to press this button,' she says, touching a silver button on her phone.

He takes the phone without saying anything.

'Thank you *so* much, you are my god,' she says again and sets her hair with both her hands, arranging it meticulously over her right shoulder Rekha-style—it never fails.

One click and the picture is taken.

'Thank you so, so, *so* much!' she says as she takes her smartphone back from the man. 'This is gonna go on Facebook as soon as this plane lands!' she says excitedly as she turns and looks at me. 'And I am gonna lie a little, I am gonna say you were my co-passenger for the journey,' she says as she gets up.

'So, what are your other favourite books?' I've got to know her taste.

'Oh, yours is the only book that I have ever read and it's *so* good!' she says rolling her eyes.

Just then a lady gets up from a seat in the front and looks at us in irritation.

'God! My mom won't let me be for even a single minute! God only knows what her problem is,' she says as the woman keeps staring at her angrily.

'Coming, Mom,' she calls back with frustration evident in her voice.

'I've got to go now,' she says, turning back to me. 'This is the best thing that has ever, ever, *ever* happened to me. You have no idea how thrilled I am right now.' She extends her hand.

I get up to shake hands with her; my other hand itching to— Suddenly, the plane hits an air pocket. God is on my side. I snake my arm around her waist. To 'support' her so she does not lose her balance.

'Jeet Obiroi!' she gasps. 'That was so inappropriate! Why would you do that? Why would you squeeze my butt like that?' she demands, looking at me wide-eyed. She is clearly flabbergasted.

I look into her eyes and smile, 'If I hadn't done that, then my card with my personal phone number would not be in your back pocket right now.'

3

Meanwhile, at a school in Dwarka, New Delhi, like every teenager, he wants love in his life—Karun

'In sooth I know not what Will Shakespeare is trying to say here. It wearies me, you say it wearies you?' I say, pushing my wind-ruffled hair back with my hand as I close my copy of *The Merchant of Venice*. And what was his huge obsession with the idea that love only makes you sad? I don't buy that at all! Falling in love only makes you smile all the time. It gives you a *new* reason to live.' This is the absolute truth. Ever since I have got to know Lovanya, the sun shines brighter in my sky. Her face is the first thing that appears in my mind when I wake up each day and that makes me feel like I am floating on clouds. In fact, she is the reason that I am sitting here, at this very spot with my friends right now. This is not where we usually have lunch during recess. This is the place where Lovanya has lunch every day with her four best friends. And today I am going to ask her to go with me for a movie. She is a sucker for action flicks and I am going to take her to watch

The Avengers. Ishan, who is *my* friend, is a good friend of *her* friend Deepti. So, the links are all in place. It won't even seem like I am piling on. I feel the two movie tickets lying in the breast pocket of my white school shirt with my hand to make sure they are still there and have not vanished like things do when we need them the most.

I see her coming, walking on the cool green grass in all her ravishing glory. My heart jumps. Yet I pretend that it does not matter to me at all.

She sits close to where we are sitting and, in less than a minute, Deepti comes and stands in front of us.

'Hi!' she says to Ishan.

'Hi!' he replies, with a glowing smile. To be honest, we are not here for me as much as we are here for Ishan. He and Deepti are almost something of an item and this is his way of meeting her every day. I am only tagging along, not really letting anyone know what's on in my mind. We are a group of three studs the whole school worships and we call ourselves the Troop of Rock, irrespective of the idea that it may or may not actually mean anything. The other two, Ishan and Gaurav, are very nice kids, but both are blabbermouths. Gaurav, in fact, is so donkey-dumb that he once actually went to our English teacher and told him that we call him the Dirty Dragon. The whole class had to face the Dragon's wrath. But it's not really fair to blame us. I mean, what other name can one give him when his mouth stinks all the time, his clothes are always soiled and his nails are long and dirty? And he is perpetually angry. His words are like fire—they burn you.

Anyway, coming back to the point. I don't like sharing my inner thoughts. I prefer to keep secrets. So, no one here knows about the tickets or my movie plan.

'Did you finish the Second World War chapter in your history class? I need the notes. I didn't understand a word of it. And your notes are really good,' Deepti says awkwardly, trying her best to sound casual.

'Yeah, we are done with it. I mean … we still have to cover the chapter in class. But I have already studied it and made notes.'

Deepti looks at him with an admiring smile.

He is lying. He has not made the notes and neither has he studied that chapter. He always uses his elder sister's notes and circulates them as *his* and hence this glory. His sister is a topper so the notes are always good. And how stupid is Deepti anyway? She can't understand WWII? It was a war! Who can't understand a war? I can write a five-thousand-word paper on it right now if you ask me. Hasn't she seen all those movies?

'Hey Lovanya, shall we join Ishan for lunch here today?' Deepti turns around and asks.

'Sure,' Lovanya says, forcing a lovely (but clearly pretentious) smile on her face. She's got style man!

She is sitting right in front of me eating a deliciously fresh-looking mint sandwich. No one in the entire school looks as beautiful as she does in the white shirt-grey skirt uniform. I look at her, taking care not to stare at her—that would only make things weird.

'We are in class ten now. We are supposed to be able to

answer the big questions of life,' Gaurav suddenly speaks up. 'What are your plans for life? What is it that we all want to do with our lives?'

Before I can open my mouth, Deepti says, 'I want to become a journalist. I want to bring about a big change in this world.'

How illusionised can people be? She does not understand a word of WWII and she wants to become a journalist who will bring about a *big change*!

'I want to become a stunter! It's the next big thing,' Ishan says excitedly. It's a term that he has invented himself, just like I have invented illusionised. It actually means a stuntman—one who does big stunts with bikes and all.

But I am not interested. I have listened to his dreams a thousand times. I only want to know what Lovanya dreams of doing. And it's not only me. We are all looking at her, waiting for her to speak.

Her beautiful lips part most elegantly. 'My dreams are not that complicated,' she says as she makes eye contact with us. 'I only want to act as an extra in a big-budget Hollywood disaster movie. I want to run screaming as a hideous and gigantic monster tramples all over the city of New York.'

'That is so cool!' I can already picture her running and screaming with dust smeared on her pretty face as a majestic building crashes behind her, blowing a cloud of dust.

Okay, this is the time to make my move. With complete style and panache, I say, 'Funny you mentioned it coz I have tickets to the biggest superhero-disaster movie of all time—*The Avengers*. Would you like to come along?'

She smiles as her friends look at her questioningly.

'Hey, you never told us you had tickets?' Gaurav jumps in.

Someone shut him up, please!

'I was just going to,' I say as I look back at Lovanya.

'Can my friends come?' she smiles.

'Sure,' I say confidently.

God! Help me get the tickets.

4

His publisher may be cheating him big time and there might be a thousand other problems, but at least he has the love of his life with him—Rohit

'Ah! I am flying!' A giddy-with-excitement Rose DeWitt Bukater exclaims to a smiling Jack Dawson. Then they entwine their arms and Jack sings, 'Come, Josephine, in my flying machine …' Nisha puts her arm around me, rests her head on my shoulder and sighs. I kiss her lightly on her head and lean back in my chair. With big, ugly 3D glasses on, we are watching *Titanic* in 3D. It's our favourite movie of all time and we *needed* to see the re-released 3D version! Moreover, it's Nisha's last evening in town and it was critical that we celebrated in a big way. Both of us couldn't think of a better way than this.

They have started kissing on the screen and someone from the audience lets out a long, sharp whistle.

'Rohit,' Nisha looks up and says.

'Yes?' I ask.

'Can you whistle like that once?'

Okay, embarrassing moment detected. I know what she means and I don't know how to do that. But I immediately curl my lips and let out a soft whistle.

'Not like that,' she says as she cuddles against my arm, 'the louder one.'

I must not do this, I must not do this!

I put my two fingers in my mouth, roll my tongue back and let out a powerful blow of air. But there is no sound, only a loud whoosh of air and everyone sitting around turns to look at me.

'It's okay,' she says, holding my hand and interlocking her fingers with mine. 'You are still the best,' she says and kisses the back of my hand.

~

If you haven't got it yet, Nisha is my girlfriend. The movie is over and we are walking on the street. It's late evening and yellow sodium-vapour lamps light the street market that is mostly winding up. As we pass through, holding hands, the tempting aroma of food wafts out from the food joints that are still active.

'Each time I watch this film, it gives me new inspiration,' Nisha says.

'The movie makes me feel the idea of love like no other movie,' I press her hand tight.

'I am getting ideas for creating a new collection,' she says.

Nisha is an artist. She paints. And her paintings sell extremely well too. Last month, one of her pieces was picked for

95k. And that's only because she is so good with what she does. Once, an art critic, considered brutal by everyone, described her work as 'fantastic and playful that gives you glimpses of another world'. Five of her contemporaries stopped talking to her after that. She has just signed a contract for a residency project for which she needs to go to Mumbai for a few months and that's why it's her last evening here with me.

'How's your third book coming along?' she asks.

'It's going on fine. It's just that I can't find my ending.' I am writing a romance-thriller and I have no clue on how to bring the end together. At times, I wake up in the middle of the night, believing that I have it. But when I write it down I feel like a total idiot at how lame it actually reads. Right now, if you ask me, I don't think I am ever going crack it. I am going to grow old and look like one of those grey-haired, long-bearded characters from *The Lord of the Rings* and will still be scratching my head and searching for an ending to the story.

'It's going to come to you. Trust me on this.'

'Yes.' I sigh.

'Any news from your publisher about the release of your second book?'

'I called him yesterday. He said printing was delayed because of the rains. The paper got wet or something like that. It's already been delayed by a month. I don't know what he is up to. Anyway, I have asked him to inform me when the copies reach him. I have talked to some journalists to review the book. Let's hope they throw some good light on it.'

I don't want to talk about this. I don't want to talk about all this tonight. My life is messed up like the tangled ribbon of an audio cassette that seems impossible to unravel. But right now, I just want to forget everything. Right now, I want to think that there is nothing wrong in my life whatsoever.

'Rohit,' Nisha looks at me.

'Yes?' I ask.

'Who do you think is the most beautiful woman ever? Not looking for a flattering answer here, looking for your opinion.'

We are quite frank with each other—we accept that both of us can find other people beautiful and attractive.

'Audrey Hepburn,' I say without hesitation. It's only once in a while that god creates a perfect face. Last time he did that, it was Audrey's.

'And who do you find most attractive?' I ask.

'Chris Hemsworth. He totally rocked in *Thor*!'

Okay, and I look nothing like him.

'I am such a loser. You are going away tomorrow and I am so broke that I can't even buy you a nice present,' I say.

'It's only poor love that needs the support and strength of money. The most precious thing one can give another is time.' She kisses me on my shoulder. She is some seven inches shorter than me and can reach only my shoulders. And I love it when she does that.

'Besides, you are going to nail that job interview tomorrow. Then you can buy me all the presents to satisfy yourself. Teaching is not that underpaid a job anymore.'

I warp my arm around her waist and hold her tight as we walk.

She looks up at me, wrinkles her nose and says, 'What do I need to do to make sure you never leave me?'

'Learn to play "Moon River" on the guitar like Audrey in *Breakfast at Tiffany's*,' I joke.

She smiles and there is a comforting silence. She is a true artist. Whenever she watches a movie or a play or reads a book that moves her, she lives it till it stays with her. Right now, she is living the immortal love from *Titanic*. Her life is driven by drama and I love her for that.

'And what would I have to do?' I smile.

'Learn to whistle with your fingers like those taporis in the cinema hall.'

5

Excited with the happenings in his life, someone is making movie plans and is flirting—Karun

I had to dodge her friends and so I did. I texted her in the morning:

```
Bad news. Show houseful, no more tickets
available.
```

To that, all the reply she sent was:

I know what that means; it means she is sad but she is coming. For if she was not coming, she would have written that.

I am standing outside the entrance to the cinema hall. It is five minutes to the show and she is gonna make it any moment now. I have my eyes trained on the door as people keep pouring in. See, there she is, wearing a yellow T-shirt and a denim skirt.

Yes!

No wait, that's not her. Damn it!

It's seven minutes past show time and she is still not here. I guess what her emoticon meant was that she was not coming. But I can't waste my ticket. And there is no point wasting the other ticket either. I pull out my cell phone and type a message for Ishan:

```
One spare ticket for Avengers. Be at DT City
Centre. NOW!
```

~

I know she's online everyday at eight. There's only five minutes to go. If she becomes visible today, it will mean she likes me and wants to take it slow. But if she comes online and is invisible, that will mean that she is avoiding me. In that case, I will have to revise my strategy which would involve major brain work. But it's okay—all for love.

It would have been amazing to watch the movie with her. It was the ultimate superhero–disaster movie ever. She would have loved it. She could easily have been an extra in the climax of the movie too. I even imagined her in the movie in a place or two towards the end.

It's exactly 8 p.m. and the messenger pops an alert.

LOVANYA WHATSINAME is online.

Ha ha, only playing hard to get. I like it.

Carnivore Karun: Hi.

Lovanya Whatsinaname: Hey.

Carni: What's up?

Lova: Am so sorry yaar I could not come for the movie!

Carni: It's okay. Not a problem.

Lova: I hope you understand. Mom would have killed me had she got to know I went alone for a movie with a guy.

Carni: Ya, I know. The movie was great though.

Lova: Ya, I am sure. Too bad I missed it.

Carni: Though it would have been even better had you been in the next seat.

Lova: ☺

Carni: ☺

Lova: Hey Karun, wanted to ask you something.

Carni: Sure.

Lova: That day, when you asked everyone what they wanted to do in their lives, you never told us anything about what you want to do with your life.

Carni: ☺ Because my friends don't have brains. They are all stupid and are completely unaware of themselves. They don't even know what they should actually do with their own lives.

Lova: Hmm, so are you gonna tell me or do you think I don't have any brains too ...

Carni: ☺ I want to become an author. The biggest author India has ever seen—the king author!

Lova: Wow! So I am chatting with a future celebrity right now.

Carni: ☺

Lova: I won't have to wait in a long Q for your autograph when you become famous?

Carni: Not if you don't mind sitting on the chair next to me when I sit and sign books for others.

Lova: ☺ So this is how you flirt. Interesting.

Carni: Do you like my style?

Lova: It's hard to say.

Carni: Can I ask you a personal question?

Lova: ☺ It's hard to say.

Carni: Have you ever had a boyfriend?

Lova: And you expect me to answer that question?

Carni: ☺ Yes.

Lova: Nope, never had one.

Carni: ☺ And you expect me to believe that?

Lova: As flattering as your impression about me might be, this is the truth.

Carni: ? You can't be serious! Such a beautiful girl! The guys from the whole school are after you and you are saying you've never had a bf?

Lova: What's that got to do with me having a bf?

Carni: No one ever proposed to you?

Lova: None that I didn't ignore.

Carni: And you never liked anyone either?

Lova: There was a guy in the seventh standard. But he never said anything and neither did I.

Carni: Who is he?

Lova: LOL! Relax, he is not in our school anymore. His dad got transferred that year itself.

Carni: Ok, but who was he?

Lova: You remember Rahul?

Carni: Yes, I do. Hmm ... Interesting. BTW, did I tell you I have already started writing my first book?

Lova: LOL! So the Q and A is finally over.

Carni: ?

Lova: Nothing. You were saying—your book.

Carni: Yes, did I tell you I have started writing my first book?

Lova: ☺ No you didn't.

Carni: It's a love story.

Lova: Is it? What's the story like?

Carni: It's about this boy who has been in love with a girl for the past six years and decides to write a story about how she is his angel for life.

Lova: Interesting. And does this girl also turn down his offer to go and watch a movie with him?

Carni: She does. ☺

Lova: Karun, you know something?

Carni: What?

Lova: You flirt good.

6

Every grown-up needs to get a job. That is the hard truth of life he's facing (though it makes him want to scream)—Rohit

I am totally going to nail this interview and I have no doubt about it. I didn't graduate from the fourth-best fine arts college in Asia for nothing. My days of penniless misery are over and done with. I will be able to buy everything I have ever wanted!

The university where I have come for the job interview is huge. They describe it as a 'sprawling campus knit into the periphery of the busy urban fabric of the city that stretches over 600 acres'. (!!!) I locate block number 8A and hurry to room number 306 where I am supposed to report for the interview.

It looks more like a mall than anything else. There are escalators running all over the place and chic girls are sitting in little black dresses with their hair tied up in buns. There is a row of futuristic looking desks and one of them reads 'Inquiry'.

'Hi,' I walk over to the desk. 'Here for an interview.'

She nods sophisticatedly and asks, 'Teaching?'

'Yes.'

She whispers something into the sleek twig like mouthpiece lining her cheek, looks at me and says, 'Room number 104. This way.' She directs me to her right.

It's a super neat, stingingly white room with only four chairs and one table—three chairs with three people sitting on them on one side and one vacant chair on the other. The room is so white that I feel my breath will dirty everything. I meekly walk in as if the whole room is pushing me down and sit on the chair. Nobody speaks and the ten seconds that pass feel like a year.

I look up at the three people sitting in front of me. All of them are busy going through the files in their hands. One of them is a short-haired, sharp-eyed woman who looks like a keen professional. Another is a repulsively fat, middle-aged man spilling out of his chair. He looks like a chunk of kneaded dough smashed on a chair. He reminds me of that gross *Star Wars* character . . . what was he called? Oh yes! Jabba, Jabba the Hutt. There is an old man sitting on the third chair who has no flesh on his face and looks like a skull. It's impossible to figure out any expression on his face.

After a full minute of my heart thumping loudly, the lady finally speaks up. 'Interesting profile you have here. You have been working as a freelance professional graphic artist for three years. And you are planning to take up teaching now. Any specific reason?' she asks as she looks up from the file she is holding and fixes her gaze on me.

The first thing that comes to my mind is: Coz I need the money! Most intellectual people don't respect those who work only for money; it's the most widely believed lie. I quickly rejig my thoughts, smile and say, 'Because I love to interact with people. I like to understand them. It's one of the things that I … like.' And that's not a lie. That's totally true.

The Jabba guy is chewing something and glaring at me as if he wants to burn me to ashes with his laser eyes or something and I am imagining the old guy looking at me stunned.

'So why this sudden change of heart? Why teaching all of a sudden?' Jabba asks with a frown.

Why is he in attack mode? What's wrong with him? I watch him chewing continuously and feel a wave of irritation rising inside me.

I look at him, smile and say, 'I have always believed, sir, that to teach, one needs to gain a certain amount of knowledge and experience. I did not feel ready before.' This and only this is the truth.

'And you think you have gained enough experience and knowledge?' he asks as he looks at me with almost disgust in his eyes.

'Learning is … is an endless process,' I stammer.

There is silence. I begin to sweat.

After an excruciatingly long time, Jabba raises his ugly head again. 'Rohit, you have come here for a job,' he says as he makes a face and looks sideways. 'Convince me you have any kind of intellectual spine.'

All right, this is it. I came here to get a job. Not to be humiliated by these three assorted peculiar beings. If they don't want to give me the job, FINE! They have no right to insult me like this. Jabba can take his job and shove it up his

ass! And I am going to just get up and leave. Not even going
to tell them why or whatever. That will be like a smashing slap
on his face. YES!

'Why don't we have a demonstration of a quick seminar?'
the professional lady asks, looking at the other two men.

'Sure, if you want that,' Jabba says without looking up from
the file in his hand.

'You are here to teach fine arts, right? Give us a quick mock
seminar for *The Scream* by Edvard Munch.'

'Sounds good,' the lady tells Jabba and then looks at me.
'Why don't you stand up and deliver it, like you would in a
class?'

I get up and stand there gobsmacked, without a clue as to
what to do. By god! I feel so dumb—I don't know anything! I
feel someone has vacuumed all the air from the room and I can't
breathe. What scream painting are they talking about? Right
now *I* feel like screaming—Hey, wait a minute! I know which
painting they are talking about. It's the one with that Paa-like
man on the bridge! It's one of my favourites! Suddenly I can
breathe again. I give out a sigh of relief and speak confidently.

'Do I really need to describe it? I mean I feel exactly like
that character in the painting right now. Don't I look like him
too?' I say as I drop my jaw and try to imitate the expression,
attempting to lighten the situation, but all three panellists look
at me blankly, completely unamused.

Okay, clearly none of them fancy jokes. I quickly need to
say something seriously academic and sound like a snobbish
art critic, using bombastically big words.

'As we all know …' Bad start! Bad start!!! '*The Scream* is

one of the most iconic pieces of art in the recent history of art. Even people who have not seen it have seen it. The use of the most appropriately selected colour palette along with the genius brushstrokes breathe life into the painting.' I could have explained the painting so much better if I had had a picture of it right now. 'Some people compare the smooth and dancing lines of the painting to Van Gogh's *Starry Night* but I think they both are far apart.'

Good, this is going good. All of them are listening to me and are not looking at each other as they have been since the beginning of the interview.

'… and while we are at it,' I continue, 'I would like to put in my personal insight about the effect and influence of the painting on pop culture—the antagonist of the biggest mega blockbuster slasher-movie franchise of its time, *Scream*, starring Neve Campbell, Courteney Cox and Drew Barrymore in a shockingly short role, was also developed from the character from the painting.' Who says watching movies is a waste of time? Had I not seen the movie, I would have never been able to draw a connection between the two arts. I look at them for their reaction as I am done with the 'mock seminar' but they seem to be expecting more and have their eyes fixed on me. So I add hesitantly, 'And … if you follow *Doctor Who*, there was an episode called "Silence" with the Eleventh Doctor which had an alien, who I believe was also developed from this very character.' Okay, they got to be insane if they still expect me to go on.

I look at the professional lady with eager eyes and she says after five seconds of silent staring, 'Please sit, Rohit.'

I smile and take a seat. I feel so tired and drained that I want this interview to end this instant.

She marks something in the file in her hands and says, 'Would you please let us know why you want to join this organization?'

Oh brother!

7

While others are struggling for things they need to do, a budding author is gearing up to become famous—Karun

I have read it all—what they call commercial Indian fiction. And it's all trash! Be it national bestselling authors like Rohit Sehdev and Jeet Obiroi or nobodies like Vivek Nagpal and Tarun Sahni, there is nothing special about any of their books. They've written nothing that I can't write. In fact, I can write much better than all of them. Rohit only does lame stuff about day-to-day happenings and tries to write what he calls 'an innocent love story', but completely fails. His slice-of-life novel is only a slice of crap if you ask me. And what is his huge obsession with his evil boss anyway? He seriously needs to get over it. Jeet Obiroi writes with this horny dude who can't relax his dick even if he wants to and only wants to run his hands up hot girls' skirts. Vivek and Tarun have both made these lame attempts at writing and glorifying what seems to be their own stories based on their own college lives but have failed miserably. There is no sense of humour in their books and the structure is totally flawed. After reading their novels, only one thing comes across clearly—their obsession with porn, sex, alcohol and drugs. They both went from small towns to these big colleges where they were exposed to new things and believe that is what life is all about. They think they are the kings of the world. It's a shame such books are even getting published. It's a disgrace. No wonder the media is writing terrible stuff about such books and is ripping them apart.

Anyway, as a gesture of respect, I must drop in mails to Rohit S and Jeet O and tell them how much I 'enjoyed' their work. If nothing else, at least their books sell. Even otherwise, I must make friends with my future contemporaries—it's all a game of contacts these days.

8

For some relationships, distance may not be a problem—Rohit

Dear Sir,

I am Karun Mukharjee from Noida and I am
your biggest fan EVER! I have rea your book
*Those Things in Everyone's Life, Big and
Small* FIFTEEN times! It is the best book
ever!!!!!!!!!!!! It is the first book I ever
read and it got me hooked to reading. In
fact, that book is really close to my life.
I felt I was reading the story of my own
life when I was reading your book. THREE
CHEERS FOR THE GREATEST BOOK EVER!!!!!! KEEP
WRITING!!!!!!!

Your biggest fan what-so-ever,
Karun Mukharjee

Fan mail is fan mail. No matter how good or bad your day is, fan mail will always give you a high. Although it's time for me and Nisha to video chat on Skype, I sit down to write a quick reply to this new 'biggest fan ever what-so-ever' dude.

```
Dear Karun Mukharjee,
    Thank you so much for such a cheerful and
energy-filled mail. Love your spirit. I am
thrilled to know that you enjoyed my work
so much.
    Wish you all the best for your future.
    Warm regards,
    Rohit Sehdev
```

I am about to click on send when a pop-up flashes on my screen saying, 'Nisha calling…' Her picture beams cheerfully at me.

I quickly hit the send button and take the call. This is how we have been keeping in touch these days—we video chat. We actually *see* each other every day and don't even feel we are away from each other.

'Hello,' I say, setting the headphone on my ears.

'So, Mr Professor, how are you?'

'I am good, how are you?'

'Oh, I am good Mr *Sexy* Professor,' she says in a husky voice. This is a game she likes to play every now and then. She will give me new names and add sexy to it each time. I think it's her way of making fun of me but she always says she can never understand why I feel I have no sex appeal.

'It's not professor, its assistant professor by the way.'

'That's even better; it makes you younger and *sexier*.'

'Ahem,' I pretend to clear my throat. 'So, how was your day?'

'Oh, it was super!' Thank god she is back to her normal self. 'We are done with experiencing the city. They gave us a tour of Mumbai and we visited all the major landmarks that I had seen so many times already by the way. We were brought to this hotel where we are supposed to stay for the next two months. It's not exactly in the city; it's somewhere outside, near a lake. It's really beautiful, secluded and peaceful. And I just love my room. It has the best view ever!'

'Great! Did you finally get a brief about what you are supposed to do?' It's quite funny actually. There is this big multimillionaire guy who has commissioned her for this art project and he hasn't revealed anything about it yet. I find it quite odd. And this is not an overreaction—anyone would be suspicious after hearing about it. The only thing I found comforting about the whole thing is that the contract mentions that if any artist wished to leave at any point during the project, he or she could do so. However, they would not hold in their favour any part of the assets gained by the project. This kind of made it clear that Nisha wouldn't be forced to do anything against her will, which was cool. If you ask me, the whole thing sounds like an Agatha Christie novel but Nisha keeps telling me that I'm overthinking this.

'Oh yes, we got the brief finally. There are a total of twelve artists from across the country. All of us will be shown a movie each week and then have to create an art piece during that week. It will be put up for auction in Paris later. This rich dude is crazy. But that doesn't make any difference to me; he is paying well.'

'Cool.'

'So, tell me, how did the whole thing go? Did you finally get to know who was who in your interview? Your messages were not really explanatory.'

Ha ha! I remembered I was whatsapping her when I was waiting for the offer letter and was bitching about Jabba—it was so fulfilling!

'Oh yes, the fat man—his name is Dr Gurinder. He's a real hotshot, masters from Harvard and PhD from Yale. He is the dean of the school. The professional lady, she is the head of the department. I didn't get any info about the old guy. Maybe he was there from HR or something—to scare people.'

'Hmm. What year are you taking?'

'I said I wanted to take the first year but Jabba glared at me and said, "No, you want the second year." As if I didn't know what I wanted.'

'Hey, did you get in touch with your publisher?'

'No, actually. I wasn't sure what I should write.'

'God! When will you ever learn? Just ask him what impression your book is running right now.'

'Hmm.'

'Are you working on your next novel?'

'Mmm, not really. But I have scrapped the previous idea. Now I am planning to write a murder mystery. So I am researching. I am reading all the Agatha Christies.'

'Hmm, and your second book is gonna be out … soon, right?'

'Right'

'Ask your publisher for the release date of your book too. Meetali is eagerly waiting to review your book.'

'That is great!' Meetali is Nisha's childhood friend. She works for a daily newspaper, the *India*.

'Okay, I have to go now. Best of luck for your new job.'

'Thank you.' I smile as I look at her on the screen.

She smiles back but there is something weird about her expression.

'What is it?' I ask

'Nothing,' she shakes her head

'*What?*'

After a short silence she asks, 'You do you remember what your college was like, right?'

9

**And the beat goes on, as someone keeps having one
successful event after another—Jeet**

You go west, you go south or you go north, there's one thing
you've got to accept hands down—there is no crowd like a
Delhi crowd. Delhi girls have dressing sense man! They know
how to look good even when they dress simply.

I am at the Red Book Store in CP and my book event is
going just perfectly. We have finished our discussion and the
panellists and I have opened the session for questions from the
audience. There are a bunch of cute girls sitting in the second
row from the front. Let's see if they ask any questions.

A girl sitting in the last row gets up and says, 'First of all, let
me thank you for having this event. It was a pleasure to have
you in front of us and hear you speak in person.' Everyone
starts to applaud and I smile, nod.

'And can I confess something? I just *love* your smile. In fact,
I decided to buy your book only after seeing your picture. I
saw your picture on the inside cover and I was like, Wow! Now

here is a handsome-looking dude, let's see what he has to say. And man, was I pleased!'

'Thank you.' I smile and nod again. I know good looks help, they always do. And that is why I am such a fitness freak. I gym regularly and make it a point to maintain a good body.

'I just have one question,' she continues, 'how much of yourself do you see in the protagonist of your book, Ravi, and how much of the story is true?'

It's quite irritating when people ask you the same questions again and again when the answers to these questions are clearly mentioned in my interviews on so many websites. But I can't offend fans—just can't afford to do so. I smile again and say, 'I think the beauty of being human is that we are all the same, and yet so different. Hence, there are definitely shades of me in the main character of my story. And, as for how much of the story is true, it's all fiction.' I have these lines memorized by heart. A friend once told me that if ever these questions were put to me, this is what I should say—with a smile.

'Thank you, sir. Thank you so much!' the girl says and sits down.

A girl sitting in the middle seat in the third row raises her hand. I look at her and nod.

She gets up and asks, 'Sir, when can we expect your next book?'

Again a question that has been thrown at me countless times. Each time I am asked this question, my mouth goes dry and my throat feels strained. *How can I tell her when my next book is coming when I have no clue myself? How the hell am I ever going to get another book out?* All the fame, all this recognition, all this fandom, I just can't lose it! I somehow manage to put on a smile and, with my heart thudding like a drumbeat, say, 'I have a few ideas in my mind but I need to work on them.'

She smiles and sits down.

The store manager comes and whispers in my ear, 'Sir, sorry to interrupt but we are running out of time. I think we should start with the book-signing session.'

'Sure,' I look at him with relief.

He makes the announcement, 'We are now open for the book-signing session. Those who want to get a copy of Jeet Obiroi's bestselling book personally signed by the author can come forward.'

This is what I love the most—sitting on a chair with long queue of people waiting to get your autograph on the book that you have written. It is so much fun, asking what is your name and adding a little smiley or a heart (depending on whether it's a boy or a girl) when they ask you to *make it special*.

The response is phenomenal here in Delhi. And it has to be. This is where my books sell the most. I have already signed fourteen books and there are still people waiting.

Someone hands me a copy of my book and says, 'I am your biggest fan, sir.'

'Thank you.' I smile and look at him. A boy, in his mid teens maybe.

'I have read your book more than five times, sir. There is no other popular fiction writer who can even think of competing with you. Your writing style is just … flawless. Your characters are so real and … it's mind-blowing, sir, mind-blowing…,' he says shaking his head.

'Thank you,' I smile.

'I have read all the books written by young Indian authors and I have to say all of them are less than trash compared to your book.'

'What's your name?' I ask as I turn my head to look at him.

'Karun Mukharjee, sir.'

'You are a student, right?'

'Yes, sir.'

'What school?'

'Ting Tong International Public School, Dwarka.'

'Nice,' I say and turn back to the book I have in my hands to sign it.

'I have a small request, sir,' he says as I sign the book with a special note to his name.

'Sure,' I say.

'I would like to stay in touch with you, sir. Actually, I am an aspiring author and I really need your guidance.'

'Sure, you can email me at the address mentioned at the back of the book.'

'Would you reply, sir? Because most authors just pass on email ids to get rid of their readers.'

'I don't know why they would do that. They must have their reasons. Send me a mail, I will reply,' I say.

'Thank you, sir, thank you so much!' he says as he takes his book and the next person in the queue steps forward.

10

Can going back to school actually be a nightmare for someone?—Rohit

It used to be a total nightmare and so is this! I was the biggest geek in the whole school and so skinny that people called me 'hanger'. They would laugh and pass mean comments like, 'Hey look, such nice clothes are roaming around!' I have gained some weight over the years but not any confidence. It's my first day at the job and I am shaking—literally. Even my hands are unsteady. But how bad could it be? After all, I am a grown-up and have seen more of this world than the kids I will be teaching. No, no. I must not panic. Must hold my feelings, must think about other things. Like … like the plot for my next novel, I think as I look around at the walls of the corridor I am walking in. What if the story goes like … umm . . . a teacher opens the door of the faculty hall and finds a student lying dead on the floor in a pool of blood? No, that is quite probable actually, it happens all the time—we read so many cases like these in the newspaper all the time.

No, that won't make an intriguing plot.

What if a teacher opens the door of the faculty hall one day and finds a peon lying dead in a pool of blood with a contorted expression on his face! The peon was a good-natured, fun-loving guy and everyone was fond of him. Now who would murder him? Who would want to kill *him*? Yes! This would make an interesting plot. I continue to rack my brain for the plot of my next novel as I walk to the hall where I am supposed to deliver my first lecture.

There is nothing to fear; I must not panic. It's all going to go smoothly. I am going take the class easily and they are going to think I am the coolest teacher ever, so much so that they are going call me the Smooth Operator or something smilar.

I stand outside the door, take a deep breath and push open the door.

It's as noisy and busy as jungle. I enter the classroom and close the door noisily to announce my presence but no student takes any notice. They are busy chatting animatedly. There is a set of girls sitting in the corner, one is stitting with her back towards me and the girl in front of her is throwing her head back and laughing at something she has just said. A boy at the back of the classroom is flinging a paper ball at another who is sitting in the front and seems to be fast asleep. Another girl is peacefully talking to someone over the phone. I know what I should do. I should do what teachers in all those TV shows do with such kids—snatch the phone from the girl's hand and smash it against the wall and break it *forever*. But for some reason, I do not do that. Instead, I walk up to her, snatch the phone and ask her, 'Who are you talking to?'

She looks back at me wide-eyed and baffled and says, 'My mother.'

Huh! *My mother*. I am sure she is talking to her boyfriend. I know kids these days. And she has no idea what I am going do.

'What's your name?' I ask.

'Anjali.'

'Anjali, please get one thing very clear in my class. You never, *ever* talk on the phone in my class.'

She looks back at me and does not say a word.

I put her phone against my ear and speak, 'Hello.'

'Hello,' a woman responds.

'Yes, who is this?' I say with full confidence.

'This is Anjali's mother,' she says.

Huh! As if I care? These parents spoil their kids these days. Beta, did you have your breakfast? Please have your breakfast on time. Beta, did you reach college on time? Please start getting up on time. I tell you, half the problems of today's youth would be solved if parents stopped nagging them.

'I am sorry, ma'am, but I don't allow students to talk on the phone in my class,' I say sternly.

'Actually, sir … her grandmother passed away this morning …' I can hear her breaking down.

Oh my god! I am a terrible person! I am the worst person in the whole world! Her grandmom passed away and I wanted to boss her around.

'Oh, I am really sorry, ma'am,' I apologize. 'Is Anjali going home?' I ask after a short pause.

'We are trying to figure that out, sir.'

'Oh, okay. I am giving the phone back to Anjali now.

And I am really sorry to hear about your loss … My heartfelt condolences … Please take care,' I say out of sheer concern.

'Thank you, sir.'

I return the phone to Anjali.

'I am really sorry to hear about your loss. You should go home,' I say softly. I just can't look her in the eye.

She looks at me and nods.

'And can you … please go out and talk on the phone?' I whisper meekly.

'Yes, sir.' She gets up and walks out of the class.

Suddenly, the class has fallen silent. I walk up to the white board and write my name on it in illegible handwriting. (That is how we are supposed to do it, right?)

'My name is Rohit Sehdev and I am your new theory of art and design teacher,' I say. It's my best shot at trying to sound serious and impressive. I have grabbed the students' attention and I must not lose it.

I go and sit on the teacher's table (not on the chair) with one foot touching the ground and the other dangling. All the cool and fun teachers sit like this; only the boring ones sit on the chair. Now I must strike up a cool conversation with the students and become their best friend. Yes, this is what I must do in my first class. I open my mouth and am about to speak when I hear a voice somewhere from behind.

'May I come in, sir?'

Irritated, I say, 'No, you may not,' and turn to see who it is. It's a guy in blue jeans and a green shirt with his collar turned up, staring at me as if he wants to kill me. He stands there for a few seconds and then walks in.

'If my permission was not required, why did you ask for it in the first place?' is what I want to say. I am outraged but must stay calm. It's my first day and the students could gang up against me and beat me up anytime. Just look at that guy sitting next to the window—he must be . . . what, well over six feet tall and looks almost like a WWE wrestler. He could knock me off in a single blow, I am sure. I must stay calm. I ignore the kid and let him take a seat.

'So, tell me,' I say as I look at the class, 'you are second-year students, right?' hoping to strike up a conversation.

Some of them nod.

'Great, let's have a round of introductions first. Why don't you tell me your names, where you are from and how you have grown up and changed in the last one year.'

No one wants to respond.

I look at the student sitting on the first seat on the right and say, 'Let's start with you.'

She stands up and is just about to speak when the kid who has just come in stands up and says, 'Ma'am, can I please go to the loo?'

Everyone bursts out laughing.

This kid is so annoying. I want to burn him alive!

Ignoring how he has addressed me, I say, 'Seriously? You guys still do that? Isn't that an ancient trick now? I know this is how you are going to bunk class and not come back.'

He stares back at me expressionless.

'I haven't even taken attendance yet,' I say.

He gives me an *as-if-I-care* look.

'Why didn't you ... erm ... finish your business before coming to the class? You were late anyway.'

No response.

'Go! How can I stop you? And why do I care anyway?' I say.

Everyone watches him go to the door, while I completely ignore his existence. Suddenly they burst into a roar of deafening laughter as he reaches the door. I am sure he must have made some rude gesture to make fun of me.

How do I control the kids now? How?!

Just then the giant sitting next to the window throws a paper ball at the sleepy kid sitting in front. The kid turns around, takes that paper ball and throws it back violently, uttering a highly evolved form of the 'F' word with a terrible prefix.

This is not good! *This is not good!*

~

What was I even thinking? There is no way I can ever control these monkeys. I am not fit to be a teacher. I am totally worthless like that. This is really terrible and I realize that I have not been this depressed in a really long time as I walk in the gloomy, dimly lit college corridor. The last time I felt this bad was when I accidently dropped my laptop in a kadhai. It was awful—I was trying to cook lotus roots (as I was totally yumstruck by the ones I had eaten at Golden Dragon) and was using my laptop to read the recipe. When I took the laptop for repairs to my electronics guy (he calls his shop Dr Laptop, by the way), he said he was really sorry but there was nothing he could do to save the fried laptop. I had spent two full weeks after that mourning over the remains of my laptop.

I go to the faculty room, and without stopping to look at anything or anyone, go straight to the cabin that I have been allotted and crash on the chair. This was a bad idea, it was all a very bad idea. This job is not for me. I cannot do this job and write my novels simultaneously. I will have to look for another job. This is not going to work. I should resign before things become too serious. Before I get more involved.

'Is Rohit here?' I hear the HOD calling. She is in her cabin, which is at the end of the faculty hall. It is the fanciest cabin with a full glass door and everything. All the other cabins are essentially only cubicles with no door whatsoever. And thanks to the location of her cabin she must have a full view of everyone and everything happening here.

'I am here,' I call out as I get up and march to her cabin. I stand by the door while she busily goes through the papers on her table.

'Please, *please*, sit down,' she says.

I sit down like a robot.

'How did your class go?' she asks.

She is going to fire me! She is going to fire me if she gets to know how terrible I was at handling the class today.

What should I say? Should I say that everything is just fine and so under control that it could not be any more under control? Should I lie and try to save my job?

'It went … pretty bad actually. I was unable to handle the kids.' I cannot lie. And what if she already knows what happened? What if she has spies? What if someone has reported to her already?

She looks up, takes off her glasses and fixes her gaze at me.

'You are not planning to quit your job, are you?'

Oh my god she is a card reader, I mean a mind reader! She has supernatural powers!!

'I was not able to handle them, ma'am. I was not able to impart any kind of knowledge to them at all. I am a terrible teacher!' I break down.

She looks at me gravely and says, 'Do you really think so?'

'Yes, ma'am,' I say affirmatively as if she is an army major or something and I a soldier.

'Okay and why is that?'

'Because they were such … animals!' I say angrily with my teeth clenched as images of those misbehaving morons come back to me. I am so angry again I want to break things. I had taken time out and had gone to teach them, to introduce them to ideas and facts they were not aware of. And all they did was hoot and shout and insult me! Teaching is the biggest favour anyone can do for anyone. I had spent one full evening preparing this lecture and this is what I got? Did they even realize what they were missing out on by treating their education like this? This time is never going to come back and they are going to be idiots for the rest of their lives.

She clasps her hands on the table and starts to speak with a firm mouth, 'I think this is exactly the reason why you are appropriate for this job.'

I shoot her a confused look.

'Many of the teachers here believe that the students' behaviour here is normal. So, for them, the idea of improving their behaviour is out of the question. But since you find their behaviour inappropriate, you will do something to improve it.'

I listen to her dumbstruck.

'Students these days are different,' she continues as I sit there listening to her, feeling like part of a movie scene where a super-experienced teacher bestows her knowledge on a young fresher. 'Don't try to control them. If you do that, it will backfire. Show them the direction in subtle, indirect ways and set them free. And you will see that they will all start doing exactly what you want them to do. They are very intelligent, you will see.' She looks at me with shining eyes. 'Being a faculty comes with a kind of magic attached to it.' She is saying what I believe in but for some reason I don't think she is right as far as these students are concerned. I don't think these beasts would be any good if they were to be set free. But now I do feel that they need me. And I do think I should try to handle them again.

11

Some people have nightmares, for some reasons no one knows—Jeet

The press conference had begun. The media was now supposed to ask questions of Jeet Obiroi—the author of the phenomenal bestseller *If I Would Not Have Met You . . . I Would Have Died*. It would not be an exaggeration to say that almost every teenager in every metropolitan city had read and loved his book. Was it because of his openness about teenage sexuality and sexual desires or because it was a simple and honest love story that everyone could relate to? Critics had different points of view. They labelled, or rather shunned, this bestseller as one of the many 'bad books' written by young engineering students turned authors mushrooming all over the country and believed themselves to be the new Chirag Barots. One critic said '. . . coming from small towns with no exposure, these so-called authors have set mediocrity as their benchmark and hence are incapable of producing anything worth appreciating.'

Jeet Obiroi feared the critics. For the first few months

after the release of his book, he had received the most terrible and rude comments and reviews. It was only after he spent a hefty Rs 6 lakh on PR and promotions that the media began to soften its stance. Some papers and magazines even started talking about his book in good light. But Jeet could still not avoid a nervous tremble when a press conference started—he had been through such terrible ones.

The cameras flashed. Jeet smiled. Journalists raised their hands to ask questions. He nodded at one sitting in the front row who stood up and asked, 'Mr Obiroi, don't you feel that the protagonist of your book is very strongly driven by his physical desires, so much so that it almost seems like a mental disorder. Don't you think portraying such a character in such glamorous light will make the young readers of your book believe that such feelings are normal and it is fine to go ahead with casual sex?'

Jeet feared journalists, but he did not fear such questions. He was only afraid of what would happen if a journalist one day discovered his secret and made it public. He would have no place to run then, no place to hide. That is what he feared more than anything. But this question was nothing. He had answered many such questions in the past and was capable of answering thousands more. He smiled and looked at the journalist, 'If eighty out of hundred people have such feelings, then all I have to say is this is what is normal. Anything else is a either a pretence or abnormal. I believe that my book frees people of their inhibitions and gives them the confidence to go ahead and enjoy the pleasures of life. We as a society keep so many things under wraps, prohibit so much. Many people regret not having had those pleasures at a later age. I just talk of the natural human instincts. I believe there is nothing unnatural or abnormal about it.'

As he finished speaking more hands rose.

There was a female journalist who had left her curly hair loose, resting lightly on her shoulders. She had an enigmatic smile and her eyes were fixed on Jeet's.

He looked at her, smiled and nodded.

She got up, 'Sir, the main character in your book is a very open and honest person. He believes in expressing himself and does not hide anything from anyone. How much of yourself do you see in his character?'

Jeet's throat tightened. The look in the journalist's eyes was screaming that she knew his secret. But would she be that brutal? Would she unmask him in front of the media like this? *No one should be that cruel.*

'I believe it's impossible to keep parts of your character from entering the characters you create. So yes, those are some of my traits,' he smiled.

She flashed a cruel smile and said, 'So I can assume that you have no secrets that you would want to hide from the world?'

'Yes,' he shrugged. He looked into her eyes. She had the look of a predator. She would not spare him.

'So the fact that your book is not …'

'SECURITY!' Jeet shouted. 'SECURITY! GET THIS WOMAN OUT OF HERE RIGHT NOW!' he screamed. 'SECURITY!'

He shot up in his bed, wide awake now. It was pitch dark in his room and he was drenched in sweat. It took him a few seconds to realize that it was just a dream and his secret was still safe. He turned on the bedside light, filled a glass of water from the bottle lying next to him and gulped it down. Switching off the light, he lay down again, resting his head on his pillow. Tossing and turning, he worried: how long would he be able to protect it? How long would he be able to keep his secret?

12

**And there are some smart kids who know really well
how to direct others to work for their benefit—Rohit**

My publisher is an asshole! I have called him eight times and
emailed him thrice in the last four days but he has neither
taken any of my calls nor called me back or even replied to my
mails. I hate it when he does this, *I hate it!* I should call Nisha
and discuss it with her. Maybe she can suggest something. And
I have also not updated her with my student adventures. It's
been a full week since we had a nice long chat. I pick up the
phone and dial her number.

'Hi,' she says, sounding distracted.

'Hey! How are you?'

'Good, good. How are you?

'Good, I am good. So, what's up?'

'Oh, we just finished watching this film. It was about this
writer. Whatever he writes starts to happen around him in
reality. It was quite nice actually.'

'Wow! Great.'

'Hey, Rohit, I need to go, yaar. I *have* to sketch out an idea that is flashing in my mind right now before I lose it. Is there anything important you need to discuss?' she asks a bit agitated. She believes that creative ideas are like energy waves that keep floating around and at times pass through us. That is the only time we conceive an idea. And if we don't push that idea to transform it through our medium into art, it will leave and travel to someone else. That is why, she says, some ideas that strike me will never come back if I don't jot them down right there right then. This happens to me all the time. She feels that these are the moments when the creative gods touch our souls. And right now, I think, she is in one of those frantic moments when she feels that she will lose the idea if she does not sketch it out.

'Oh no, I just wanted to tell you how my class went and that the kids are monsters and my publisher is an asshole. But no worries. I can rant later. Or I will mail you maybe. Yeah, I will do that.'

'Okay,' she says with little laugh. I know had I been in front of her, she would have pulled my cheeks and said 'fine' with pouty lips. 'Talk to you later then, bye.'

'Bye, see you, take care.' I don't want to disconnect the call.

'Bye,' she laughs as she disconnects the call.

I put the phone aside gloomily and turn on my laptop. I am hoping that some sense has hit my publisher's head and he has replied to my (multiple) mails. But to my utter dismay, there is no mail from him. Instead, there is an email from that same kid who had mailed me a few days back.

```
OMG!!!!!!!!!!!!!!!!!!! I can't believe that
you replied! (U ACTUALLY REPLIED!!!) My most
favourite author in the whole world replied
to me!!! GOD! I still can't believe it!!!
You are the best person in the whole world!
And can I please call you bhaiya? Sir is
too formal. And you are really like an elder
brother to me ☺.
     Yours sincerely,
     Karun Mukharjee
```

What a nice, honest, pure-hearted kid! Why aren't the kids in my class like him? Civilized and … human beings most of all. I want to send him a reply right now. And why shouldn't I? It's only going to make him happy.

```
Dear Karun,
     Thank you so much for such a nice mail. I
am overwhelmed, honestly. And sure, you can
call me bhaiya ☺.
     Best wishes,
     Rohit Sehdev
```

I click on 'send' and in less than a minute a new IM window pops up on my screen.

Carnivore Karun: Thank you bro! ☺ Now that we are brothers, can I ask you for a favour?
Writing Rohit: Sure.

Carnivore Karun: I am also writing a novel and I need your help with that.

Writing Rohit: Sure, what kind of help?

Carnivore Karun: Actually when I read your first novel, I felt that it was completely my own story and I should also write a novel ;)

Writing Rohit: Cool.

Carnivore Karun: I will be dedicating this book to you ☺. Initially, I was thinking of calling it 'I Too Am A Writer'. But now I have a different title in my mind—'Please Cum To Me my Love'.

For a moment I stare at the screen.

Writing Rohit: ... Okay, but why 'cum' and not 'come'? You know the difference between the meanings of the words, right?

Carnivore Karun: LOL! No I didn't. I just googled! But I am sure no one would no the other meaning either. Besides I don't have a choice—the publisher wants it to be exactly 19 characters :p it's some numerology shit.

For this phrase, there is no other meaning of the word, just one meaning and one meaning only but I don't know how to make him understand that.

Writing Rohit: Hmm ... but I still wish you would change the title. Try another one maybe?

Carnivore Karun: LOL! It's ok, I like it this way. :p

Writing Rohit: Hmm ...
Carnivore Karun: Hey! I gtg. Will catch u later. Will mail you the chpts. Do read dem, k?
Writing Rohit: Sure.
Carnivore Karun: Cu bye.
Writing Rohit: Bye.

Poor kid, he doesn't even understand the word he is using. I am sure he still believes it can be used as short form for come. Just then a new mail pops up.

```
Dear Rohit,
    This is in reference to your earlier
mail. I will get the number of impressions
your first book is in right now and let you
know soon. As for the release date for your
second book, I will let you know as soon as
I get the books from the printer. You know
how terribly it rained yesterday. And as I
told you earlier, paper becomes moist in such
weather and it becomes difficult to print.
The roads also get clogged with water and
it becomes difficult to transport the books
as they get wet.
    Best wishes,
    D.K. Dé
```

Hmm, he does not even know what impression my first book is running. He is such a liar!

13

After this, his publisher would start flirting with him—Karun

It's all flying horse shit and I don't buy it at all. I don't believe that a manuscript should be submitted to a publisher in an email. There are so many reasons:

a) A meeting leaves (definitely) a stronger impression. They are more likely to consider and think more about your manuscript if you meet them.

b) They will be (more) aware about your existence and hence think twice before stealing or passing it on with some other name or misusing it in any other way.

c) You get to meet them and in turn get to understand them better and hence stand a better chance at figuring out how to deal with them.

I pull out my cell phone from my pocket on and open the note where I had saved the publisher's address that I copied at the bookshop from a book I didn't buy.

Yes, the address is correct but the place looks nothing like a publisher's office. It looks like a house. But they can't put the wrong address in their book, can they? There's only on way to find out—I walk in through the open door.

It looks like an average three-bedroom flat with a hall. There are huge piles of books packed in transparent plastic everywhere and there are two desks behind which two guys seem to be working. I walk over to the one sitting closer to the door (he has to be the receptionist) and ask him quite a stupid question, 'Excuse me, is this the Dash Publishers office?'

The man looks up and says, 'Yes.'

'I am here to meet the commissioning editor.' I have done my homework. This is the designation that takes all the decisions.

'I am sorry but the editorial team does not sit in the office.'

What kind of publishing house is it? *The editors don't sit in the office?*

'Okay … where can I find them? I am here to submit a manuscript.'

'Let me check,' he says as he picks up the receiver of the phone to his left, punches a single digit number and waits.

'Hello,' he finally speaks up, 'yes, there is a boy who wants to submit a manuscript … yes … yes, the one standing in front of me … yes, the one in the blue T-shirt… okay.'

He puts the receiver down and looks at me, 'The editor is not here but you can meet Mr Dé, he owns this company.'

Score!

Mr Dé's office is not particularly big. His table and chair are placed in the middle of the room and there is a bookshelf to his right which has copies of some titles.

'Good morning, sir,' I greet him.

He is smoking a cigarette that he stubs in an ashtray kept in front of him and says, 'Good morning, please sit.'

There is an odd silence for a few seconds and then I speak up, 'My name is Karun, sir, and I wanted to submit a manuscript.'

'Okay,' he nods.

I smile and place the spiral bound manuscript on the table.

'Good … and what kind of story is it?' he asks as he picks up the manuscript.

'It's essentially a love story, sir.'

'Is it *your* love story?' he says as he looks up from the manuscript, makes eye contact and smiles.

'Not really.' I must remember the mantra: All characters are fictitious and bear no resemblance to any person living or dead. Any such resemblance is merely coincidental.

'I see,' he says flipping through the pages, 'you have written it as your autobiography. So if anyone asks you, you should say it's a semi-autobiographical account of your life. People these days want to read real-life stories. It interests them more; it makes them feel they are reading something real, like someone's personal diary.'

'Okay,' I nod.

'You are a charming young boy,' he says looking at me, 'I am sure it is an interesting story.'

'Thank you, sir,' I smile. This is great! He is almost saying that he has accepted the manuscript.

'Let me go through the manuscript once. I will then forward it to the editor who will prepare an evaluation report that I will send you. Please write your email address on the first page of the manuscript.' He opens the first page of the manuscript and pushes it towards me.

'How old are you?' he asks.

'I am sixteen, sir.'

'Does the book have any sex scenes?'

'No, sir.'

'Hmm,' he lights a cigarette. 'Sex is what sells these days. If you put in some such scenes, I think it would help the sales should we decide to publish your novel.'

'Okay,' I nod. So sex is what I need to add now.

'Have you read any Jackie Collins or Shobhaa Dé books?' he asks.

'No, sir.'

'You should read them. That is the kind of thing people want to read these days.' He looks at me again and says, 'Wait, I will give you a book, you should read it.' He takes out a book from one of the drawers in his table and hands it to me.

It's a Jackie Collins and the cover has a picture of the face of a girl with her mouth wide open, licking a finger.

'Cool, sir, I will read it,' I smile.

'So,' he smiles, 'do you have a girlfriend?'

14

The dean is fat, gross and seems to have many demented sexual fantasies—Rohit

I have it all figured out. I know the who's who in my class now. There are two students whom everyone considers the ringleaders of the class. One is Pranav (the guy who came late and then went to pee) and the other is Ranova (the one who had her chair turned back towards me and was cracking jokes that made everyone throw their heads back and laugh). I just need to snub these two students (whom I hate by the way) in order to get the class in control.

I am on my way to the dean's office right now. Jabba—I still can't think of him as Dr Gurinder—has 'summoned' me for a meeting. I guess all these authority people need to be certain they have hired the right candidates—that is why all these meetings.

I knock the door and wait till I hear 'Come in.'

I push the door open to see a room that looks nothing like a dean's office should. The room is even shabbier than my own and I can see a layer of dust on the table which has some files and papers scattered all over. In the middle of the room is the dean's big table and chair behind which there is a bookrack of sorts where nothing is in order. He is sprawled on his chair, his eyes fixed on the copy of *Fifty Shades of Grey* in his hand. And I totally pretend that I have not seen where his other hand is as I do not want any kind of embarrassing situation.

'Oh, Rohit,' Jabba is startled to see me and instantly throws the copy of *Fifty Shades of Grey* on the shelf behind him.

'I was waiting for you,' he says clearing his throat. 'I thought it was the peon.'

I smile.

'Sit, sit' he says.

I sit down as he picks up an unwrapped slab of chocolate lying on his table, breaks it into half, shoves it into his mouth and offers the other half to me, 'Chocolate?'

In the process of shoving the chocolate into his mouth some semi-molten chocolate gets smeared on his lips, hand and fingers—that completely grosses me out.

'No, thank you,' I say forcing a smile.

'How are your classes going?' he asks, chewing his chocolate.

'Going fine, sir. There were a few problems in the beginning but now things are fine. I am getting the hang of it,' I nod.

'You know these students, they are *imbeciles,*' he says with his teeth clenched. 'They should be stripped *naked* and beaten up.'

Okay, this is awkward. I don't know how to react. Is he getting too influenced by the book he is reading?

We both sit for a while, looking at each other, not knowing what to say. Finally, I speak up, 'Sir, I have a class, can I leave?'

'Yes, yes. And I am sorry, yaar, if the kids misbehaved ...' he shakes his head.

'It's totally fine, sir. One of their assignments is due today. I hope they turn it in,' I smile.

'These kids are imbeciles, *imbeciles*!' he says again with his teeth clenched.

～

'You, at the back, both of you,' I say addressing the two students sitting in the last row—both have been chatting away to glory since the class started and have paid no attention at all to what I have been saying.

The boy points his thumb towards himself in a questioning gesture as if he doesn't know I am talking to him. The girl sitting next to him is giggling so hard it seems she will explode like a bomb any moment. And the two are none other than Ranova and Pranav.

'Yes, you. Would you please share the joke with us all? A little laughter is always welcome.'

'Sir, you don't want to know,' he says.

'No, seriously, I do want to know,' I shoot back.

He does not say anything and looks at me at me with a fixed angry stare. These kids, they really make my blood boil!

'Go on, tell me, what was she saying?' I probe.

Without hesitating for a moment, he blurts, 'She was saying that you are very sexy.'

The whole class bursts out laughing. I feel my cheeks turning warm and pray they are not turning red with embarrassment. I know for a fact that the only kind of sex appeal I have is negative sex appeal, like Lalu Yrasad Padav or Jabba or someone. Kids these days have no shame at all! I am totally speechless and don't know what to do. The only thing I can think of is talking about something else and changing the topic.

Just then Pranav speaks up again flashing a cocky smile. 'Sir, I told you that you don't want to know,' he says and winks at the girl sitting next to him. I want to wring his neck! I want to wring his neck and kill him!!

The class has burst into another bout of laughter.

'SILENCE!' I scream louder than I am capable of. 'If you do not shut up then I am going to rip your heads off and throw them out of the window!'

Clearly, it is a totally hollow threat and there is no way on earth I can do what I just said but surprisingly all of them have fallen silent and are looking at me kind of scared and wide-eyed.

'You had your assignment due today. Where is your submission?' I shout with fire in my eyes.

No one moves or says anything. Obviously, none of them has written any assignment. 'I want you to take out your notebooks, and write the assignment *now*! One thousand words on the development of world art in the last fifty years,' I say, looking at them like an angry hunter. They all pull out their notebooks like the meek circus animals that we used to have once upon a time, and start writing. Including Pranav and Ranova.

Huh! What were they thinking?

Just then I hear the kid sitting on the front seat whisper to the one sitting next of him, 'This class is so boring.'

~

I am reading the chapters Karun sent me and I must say they are quite nice. It's a story about a schoolboy who has been in love with a classmate for over four years. She also happens to be his neighbour. The chapters read fresh and the characters innocent. I am close to finishing the third chapter when I get an alert on my phone.

It's a Whatsapp message from Karun.

Hi bhaiya! Up for a chat?

Hmm, I am almost done. Maybe I can give my feedback. I turn on my computer and he is already online.

Carnivore Karun: Hi Bhaiya!
Writing Rohit: Hi.
Carnivore Karun: Did you read the chapters?
Writing Rohit: Yes.
Carnivore Karun: And? How were they?
Writing Rohit: They are quite nice actually. I like the energy that you have maintained. It reads very fresh.
Carnivore Karun: Yeaah!!! Thank you so much bhaiya! You have made my day!!! My most favourite author ever liked my book!!! This is the best day of my life ever!!! Thank youuuu!
Writing Rohit: It's okay.

Carnivore Karun: Thank you.

Writing Rohit: Have you sent the manuscript to any publishers?

Carnivore Karun: Yes.

Writing Rohit: Which ones?

Carnivore Karun: I sent to a few but Dash Publishers accepted.

Writing Rohit: Okay.

Carnivore Karun: So we are publisher mates too now.

Writing Rohit: ☺

Damn, he has no idea what he is stepping into. I wish I could save him.

Carnivore Karun: But there is a little problem.

Writing Rohit: What?

Carnivore Karun: The owner of the publishing house, Mr D.K. Dé, keeps forcing me to put sex scenes in the book.

Writing Rohit: How can he force you? It's your wish if you want to put such content in your book or not.

Carnivore Karun: Yes, but he says sex sells and I should do it in order to make my book sell well.

Writing Rohit: I am sorry but had I been in your place I would not have done it.

Carnivore Karun: That is why you are you bhaiya. You are the BEST!!!

Writing Rohit: ☺

Carnivore Karun: And also ... at times he ... behaves very strangely on chat.

Writing Rohit: Okay ...?

Carnivore Karun: The other day I was online and he pinged me. He was invisible so I didn't know he was online or I would have gone offline.

Writing Rohit: K ...

Carnivore Karun: He started chatting weirdly and I don't know how to say this but ... he sent me porn links.

Writing Rohit: God! That's terrible!

Carnivore Karun: Yeah. And he said I should introduce a gay character coz that's a real hot topic these days and gays are coming out in a big way.

Dé is sick. I knew he was scum but this is outrageous. He is a pervert at all possible levels. A paedophile! This kid is what, sixteen? And he is polluting his mind by forcing him to watch porn!! TERRIBLE!!!

Carnivore Karun: When I talk to him over the phone, he is all fine. But when he chats ...

Writing Rohit: Hmm ...

Carnivore Karun: Does he chat with you like this too?

Writing Rohit: No, I don't chat with him. We correspond only through emails and phone.

Carnivore Karun: Okay. Yeah, that day, it was too weird man! He started acting so strange and I didn't even know how to avoid him.

This is terrible. This guy should be sent to jail.

Writing Rohit: You could have just logged off.
Carnivore Karun: No, bhaiya, I didn't want to offend him!!!
What if he decides not to publish my book? I will be ruined!!! I
will lose the love of my life! No, no! You want to see that chat?
Writing Rohit: Okay.

Let's see how rotten this guy can actually get.

Carnivore Karun: But don't say anything to anyone about
this, ever! Please, please, please!!!
Writing Rohit: K, trust me, I understand, won't tell anyone.
Carnivore Karun: Thank you bhaiya. YOU R D BEST!

He mails me the chat and I am disgusted beyond imagination
to read it. Mr Dé is talking about how he masturbates and how
he can sustain a hard-on for a long time. He is asking Karun
how he likes to masturbate and makes fun of him by saying
that he mustn't be able to prolong it. To my utter shock, the
porn links are gay porn links.

Writing Rohit: You understand that those were gay porn
links that he sent you.
Carnivore Karun: Yes, and it was so embarrassing. The comp
in our house is in the living room and my mom was there
that time and he kept sending links.
Writing Rohit: Hmm ...
Carnivore Karun: And it is soo weird—if I call him sir or
uncle, he objects. He says that I am his friend and I should
call him by his first name ... otherwise he won't be able to

talk to me as friend.

Writing Rohit: Hmm. I hope you realize that he is not the best person.

Carnivore Karun: Yes bhaiya.

Writing Rohit: And I suggest that next time he talks to you like this you should tell him that you are not comfortable talking about all these things.

Carnivore Karun: Yes bhaiya, thank you so much. I don't know what I would have done without you, big brother ☺

Writing Rohit: You are welcome.

Carnivore Karun: I got to go now bhaiya. Thank you so much. And once again—U R D BEST

Writing Rohit: Thank you, bye.

Carnivore Karun: Byeeeeeeeeee☺

This is not right. This is not done, this is just not done! I must do something about it!

15

The sexy beast meets a stronger, sexier 'sexy beast'—Jeet

It's the usual thing—hot chicks check me out whenever I travel. I am on a train, on my way to Lucknow for my next book event and there is this really hot girl next to me who has been checking me out since she sat down. It was a good decision to select this red T-shirt I am wearing today. It highlights my guns and girls love that. But who's gonna break the ice—that is the question. Times have changed. It's not a rule anymore that guys have to make the first move. I turn my head and look outside the window, almost sure that it's now that she is going to try and strike up a conversation.

'Excuse me?'

Yes, I knew it!

'Yes?'

'Do you have a pen?'

A question with a dirty annotation, I like that.

'Of course I have one. Every man's got to have one,' I smile.

She smiles back and says, 'Can I have it then, if you really have one?'

'I can't think of a reason why you should not,' I say as I get up to take the pen from the bag kept on the shelf above my seat. I flex my well-toned triceps and make sure that my washboard six-pack abs are exposed in the process of pulling out the pen. I look at her from the corner of my eye as she catches a glimpse of my six-pack.

'Here you go,' I say, giving her the pen as I sit back on my seat.

'Thank you,' she says, taking it from my hand.

She takes a piece of paper from the bag lying in her lap and starts writing on it.

She is quite a looker I must say. Deep brown eyes, light brown hair with light curls and fair, flawless skin.

'You know what I am writing?' she asks. She knows I am looking at her.

'Nope.'

'I am writing,' she says, 'what I am going to say to my fiancé. How I am going to explain and justify this month-long, random, unplanned trip that I plan to go on before our wedding.'

'So, you're getting married?'

'Yeah.'

'If you don't mind me asking, is it a love marriage?'

'Ah, I wish! No, it's not a love marriage. It's an arranged one. I come from a very conservative family. They want to marry me off by the age of twenty-four. My mother keeps telling me that it becomes very difficult to make babies and raise them if you get married late.'

'Hmm, so this trip … where all do you plan to go?'

'Don't know. It's a random trip. I am thinking of going city hopping. Don't have anything in mind as such.'

She looks like a cool girl, free minded. Is there a chance?

'I tell you what …' I say, 'I am also on a tour of sorts. I am also going to cover a few cities. Why don't we do that together?'

She looks at me for a few seconds and says, 'Hmm, interesting. What kind of trip are you on?'

She does not know me. She does not know that I am a writer on a book tour. It would be fun to play along for a while.

'You can say it's kind of a work trip,' I smile.

'Cool. What we can do is travel together, reach a city, go our separate ways do what we want to do there, go where we like and then meet again and travel together to the next place.'

'Sounds like a plan,' I nod.

'Cool,' she jumps up, 'and I also have a to-do list that I need to complete before I get married.' She pulls out a small notebook from the bag she has on her lap and says, 'And the first thing on the list is to get rid of the stack of porn I have with me.'

I am kind of taken aback by what she says. I have never met a girl who is so open about her porn collection (if at all she has one).

'What? Why so shocked? Don't *you* have a collection? Don't *you* watch porn?' she looks at me with her eyes wide.

'I do but … anyway, forget it.'

'So, I want to get rid of this,' she says pulling out a spindle of DVDs from her bag. 'And I don't want anyone to find it in my stuff after I get married. You know how people start to judge you. And I don't want to throw it away either, that would be such a waste. It's such an assorted, tasteful collection.' She looks at me and asks, 'Would you like to take it?'

She is a smart girl. I like that. Seems we have a lot in common.

'Sure,' I smile as I look back at her, 'maybe we can watch it together. You can tell me which one's good and which one's not and why.' I wink.

'Oh, shut up,' she says, slapping my hand on the armrest as she throws her head back and laughs.

16

He is terribly disturbed to know that his publisher flirts with his authors—Rohit

Hey love,

I don't know what the world has come to. I had a chat with an aspiring author yesterday and can you believe this? The publisher, *my* publisher, sex chats with him? I am sure this was the last thing the world had to show us—*publishing couch*! Now it all is going to end, like *The Day After Tomorrow* and *2012*. We all are going to drown or burn or ... die some way. Anyway, I was really upset to know what was going on with that kid and I really want to do something about it—an exposé on this whole thing about the publisher maybe? Can your journalist friends help pull this thing off?

How's everything going at your end? How

```
are the movies turning into paintings? Do
fill me in. And you did not reply to my last
mail. Are you even reading my mails?
    Love,
    Rohit
```

~

Today is going to be an amazing day. I have come up with this super novel concept for the next assignment that is going to thrill the kids out of their skin!

I enter the classroom with hard-to-beat confidence, walk over to the teacher's table and sit in my signature style.

'So, I have been thinking over your comments about the class being boring.' I shoot a look at the kid who had whispered that day. 'And I have been thinking how to make this class interesting.'

I walk to the white board and write, '*A Handful of Nuts*'. This action of writing something on the board first and then talking about it is something I have learnt from watching episodes of *Glee*. Each time Mr Schuster does this, it looks so impressive and all the students are in complete awe.

'It's the best light read written by an Indian author and was written years before the popular *5 Point 5 One* and is way, way better than any of the popular fiction novels being written these days, about a horny guy trying to run his hand up a girl's skirt. It has the breezy feel of R.K. Narayan, has a youthful freshness to it and is actually quirky. And quite interestingly, it is something of an insight that some people might call history.'

I expect the students to look at me all happy and excited like the kids on *Glee* (and clap maybe) but they are behaving nothing like them. They are whispering and chatting amongst themselves.

I continue. 'It's written by Ruskin Bond, one of the best fiction writers of our time.' I look at them but still no sign of excitement. 'And it's not even a fat book that would scare you away.' I go on, 'You only have to read the book, analyze the story and make a painting inspired from it.'

Ravona is in the last row and I see her passing a small chit to Pranav who is sitting in front of her. He unfolds the chit, reads it, laughs, writes something on it and passes it back.

Okay, this is it! This is the greatest insult a student can ever throw at me. I have worked so hard—I have been thinking for over a week on how to make this class more interesting and this is how they behave? Not even listen when I am talking to them? This is not done, this is just not done! There is no way I am taking this. I am declaring war with Pranav now! But I am going to treat this girl differently—split them apart and make Pranav jealous. Yes, I am going to be that evil.

I march up to Ravona, who is busy reading the chit she has just received and is giggling. I take her by total surprise and snatch the chit out of her hands, startling her. She almost gives out a little scream.

What I read infuriates me like I have never been infuriated before.

Handful of nuts? I wonder how many nuts he has?? :O

And below that, in Pranav's hand, it says,

> LOL! The Nutty Professor! Imagine him in an old
> woman's get-up dropping his panties. LOL!

Okay, I seriously want to rip this girl's head off like they do
in those vampire TV shows with fountains of blood spurting
from their necks. But I must not do anything like that. These
are children and I must forgive them. Right now I must think
of ideas like Zen and people like the Dalai Lama.

I look at the girl and smile. '*The Nutty Professor* was a funny
movie,' I say as I hand the chit back. Both Ravona and Pranav
stare back at me, stunned. Score!

'Peace,' I say, 'is a powerful notion.' I walk away from
them and towards the white board. 'If we maintain peace, if
we remain calm, we can solve any problem. And with a little
bit of love added to it, we can win any heart.'

'Peace is an old fashioned idea,' I hear a boy's voice say.

After a moment of silence, I hear a girl's voice say, 'I
disagree.' I turn around and see it's Ravona. 'Peace *is* a strong
notion,' she says as she looks at me. She has a serious look on
her face. It's not the usual *I-will-never-stop-making-fun-of-you*
kind of stubborn look. It's like that shell has melted away and
the real Ravona is looking at me now. I look back at her and
smile. I understand her apology.

~

I step out of the classroom and am still a little upset actually. Why do these kids behave the way they do? What is wrong with them? I am walking to the faculty room when the HOD catches me.

'Rohit, I need to talk to you.'

Oh god! What did I do now?

'Yes, ma'am,' I say as I halt but she keeps walking, faster than my fastest brisk walk.

'Keep walking. Keep walking as I talk.'

I almost have to run to keep pace with her.

'You know Pranav from your class?'

Damn sure I do. I nod to confirm.

'He has been having certain problems lately. His behaviour has been totally off and he is getting involved in things he must stay away from.'

Oh my god! Is he a junkie?? Is he a *drug addict*?

'He needs to be put into a new environment.'

Hurray! We are throwing him out of college! Yesss!

'I had a word with his mother on the phone today. The hostel is no good for him. The environment is spoiling him further.'

She is not being specific. She is not telling me what exactly the problem is. But I understand—I can guess, I am not that dumb.

'Okay …' I nod as I walk as fast as I can to match her pace, almost panting.

'I was wondering if you could take him to your place for a few days. I think that would be a nice change for him. Is that possible?'

No! *No!!* How do I say it? *How do I say it??* Will she fire me if I say no?

'Hmm …' I stutter as I struggle with my thoughts.

'Great, then I will talk to his mother and see if he can stay with you for the rest of the semester. He is a great kid. Only needs to be loved a little,' she says as she gains even more speed and vanishes into a room. I stand there struggling to get over my perspective about the kid. I'm still thinking about the last line she said when I am startled by a voice.

'Rohit?'

'Yes,' I jump. It's Jabba.

'What was she telling you?' he says, chewing whatever he has in his mouth.

'Nothing, sir, we were just discussing a student.'

'Was she saying anything that concerns me? What was she saying about me?'

'Nothing, sir, She didn't say anything about you.'

What's wrong with him? Why would he ask me that?

'Okay, okay. And please, yaar, if the kids misbehaved I apologize. They are criminals. *Hardened criminals.*'

'It's okay, sir,' I laugh.

'Please, yaar,' he says, shaking his head as he walks off.

God! What is with people here??

17

Stealing is (obviously) okay, as long as no one gets to know about it—Karun

I wait for the day I can find out why all the classrooms are designed so dull and what the architect was thinking when he designed this classroom in particular. Just look around. The windows are on the wrong side so there's a terrible glare on the blackboard. One door opens so horribly close to the benches that it is kept closed during class, thus cutting the light that comes into the room. I will never understand why they will put only that ugly green paint up to three feet all around on the walls. And only so that no one can blame them for being boring, they have given this one wall for the 'cheerful' and 'bright' charts and drawings made by the students.

The first period is on and as bad as things are, the Dirty Dragon is teaching us. It's the English class and we are studying Shakespeare's *The Merchant of Venice*. I just don't get the point of this play. These days no one is that stupid. If they want to kill you, they will make sure they mention flesh *and* blood as the forfeit. It's not the 1500s anymore. The human mind has evolved.

To my relief, I am sitting on the best seat where no teacher ever notices you—two seats beyond the middle seat in the row. Teachers are always busy looking at the people either sitting on the front seats or at the last seats. This region, as a rule, is left unmonitored. The Dragon is going on and on about the 'famous' casket scene where Bassanio chooses the stupid lead casket and jumps like a monkey for his win. I have seen the movie already and have read the play too. There is nothing new that this bad teacher with terrible hygiene is going to tell me—I know it all already! That is why I am writing this poem for Lovanya who is sitting in the next row just one bench ahead of mine.

> *All day I'm walking in a dream,*
> *I think about you constantly.*
> *Just like an ever flowing stream,*
> *Your memory haunts me constantly.*
> *Shadows fall and I try to drive you from my mind,*
> *So you're no longer near to me.*
> *But my heart sees you there with me,*
> *Every sunset you share with me.*
> *The rain that patterns through the tree,*
> *Reminds me of you constantly.*
> *Your name is whispered by the breeze and love birds,*
> *Bring your song to me.*
> *Just as same as each star keeps burning,*
> *In the sky your flame will stay a flame in me.*
> *A flame that burns so bright,*

Not only through the night,
But constantly.
Tho we may be far apart,
You're constantly deep in my heart.

It's not my original work, though that would have been more meaningful and even more beautiful. But I don't have that much time. This is an old song by Cliff Richards. But I am sure she mustn't have heard of him or his songs, so it's okay to write it. I fold the piece of paper and take a deep breath, bend a little towards Lovanya and blow, tickling her on the side of her neck. She turns back to look at me with her divinely beautiful eyes. I smile and give her the piece of paper. She silently takes it, smiles and then folds it, puts it in her book she has open in front of her and looks at the Dirty Dragon again.

'Karun,' I hear the Dragon and I immediately look away from Lovanya and pay attention to him.

'I am not going to create a scene by asking Lovanya to give me the piece of paper you just handed her and read it out loud and embarrass both of you. That would be a pure waste of time because kids as stubborn as you are never going to improve,' he says with a hint of anger in his voice.

'Thank you, sir,' I say as the whole class starts laughing.

He stares angrily at everyone and they all shut up.

'I am only going to ask you to quote the last line from the play that we just discussed,' he says and looks straight at me. In fact, everyone has turned around and is staring at me.

I look at him and don't say anything. I just don't like this guy!

'Your choice, Karun, you tell us what we were discussing or do us all a favour. Let us study without the disturbances you create and please leave the class,' he says with his nostrils flaring.

That is a way better option than sitting in this boring class. Besides, I have accomplished what I came to this class for—given Lovanya the poem. I get up and start walking towards the door when I hear the Dragon say, 'People like you, Karun, turn out to be the biggest losers in life. Your hollow attitude and shallow nature is not going to take you far. You will be failure all your life and will be blind to the reason for that.'

What the … ?! He has no right to say any of that. And what does he think of himself? Being an English teacher, he is worthless in front of me, a soon-to-be-published author. I turn around, look at him and quote: 'You that choose not by the view, Chance as fair, and choose as true! Since this fortune falls on you, Be content and seek no new. If you be well pleas'd with this And hold your fortune for your bliss, Turn you where your lady is And claim her with a loving kiss.' I say the last words as I look at Lovanya and then I look at the Dragon again. 'Act 3 Scene 2—the casket scene. That is what we were discussing. But Mr Shakespeare missed a point there. Things that glitter, don't glitter for nothing. They do have great value. Gold not only looks good, but has medicinal properties, used to cure TB in certain cases. And lead not only appears ugly to the eye, but is also poisonous,' I say as I turn and walk out of the class.

18

**When he learns that his student knows how to write
music and he does not—Rohit**

I hadn't noticed how shabby my apartment had become. It's
only now that Pranav has come with me to my place that I
notice. He is being quite well behaved today. I asked him if he
wanted to have an ice cream before we left for home and he
agreed. Maybe it was a magic ice cream—he has been behaving
rather nicely after that.

I enter my apartment, slightly embarrassed at its state. There
are books everywhere—on the sofa, on the dining table …
The place is a mess. As it is I have very little furniture. There
is only a low table in the middle of the living room. There is
low seating, next to the wall, with brown and green cushions
lying carelessly on the light-brown bedsheet among the books
and the notes I was working on last night. The door to the
balcony is closed and the setting sun is sending the lazy, retiring
evening light into the room.

'I am sorry the place is such a mess. I just don't get the time to clean it,' I explain.

'It's okay, sir-ji. You have no idea how messy my hostel room is,' he says. 'And actually messy places make me feel comfortable, it's like I am in my own room,' he smiles.

After a short pause, he says, 'Sir, my mom wanted to talk to you.'

'Oh, okay.'

He pulls out his phone from his pocket, dials a number and speaks, 'Hello, mom. Yes, talk to him.'

He looks at me and hands me the phone, visibly anxious. I am no less nervous. How am I supposed to talk to my student's parents? Last time, when I talked to one, it was a complete disaster. What should I say? Should I complain about his behaviour or should I just say that he is a nice, happy fellow? I clear my throat and speak into the phone, 'Hello.'

'Good evening, sir,' his mother says courteously.

'Good evening, ma'am, how are you?'

'I am good, sir, how are you?'

'Good, good. I am good.'

'I wanted to thank you for such a generous favour. Pranav really needs supervision right now,' she says.

'Not a problem at all, ma'am,' I smile.

'Pranav was telling me that he used to misbehave in your class. I have given him a good thrashing. I apologize for his behaviour and assure you that he will never behave like that again.'

'It's okay, ma'am.'

'Pranav's biggest problem is that he is very lazy. He just needs to be pushed a little to make him work.'

'I will keep that in mind, ma'am.'

'Thank you, sir. And if this boy troubles you even a bit, just let me know. I will set him right.'

'Sure, ma'am.'

'Okay, sir, thank you so much.'

'Thank you, ma'am,' I say and she disconnects the call.

I give the phone back to Pranav and see him looking at me nervously again. After a short silence he says, 'Sir-ji, can I please request you for something?'

'Okay,' I say.

'If you ever get angry with me, you can scream at me, beat me, but please don't tell my mom.'

I look at him and can't resist smiling—he is actually behaving like his real self with me.

'Okay.'

'Promise?' he asks.

'Okay.'

'*Promise?*' He looks at me with eyes as wide as saucers; he wants me to say the word.

'Okay, okay. Promise.' My god! Kids!!

He looks around trying to find a place to sit when he sees the three-string guitar lying in the corner of the room.

'Sir-ji, do you know how to play the guitar?'

'Oh no, it's a friend's. He was kind of getting rid of it when he was moving to Bangalore, wanted to take as little stuff as possible. Wanted to buy a new fancy one, so left this one with me.'

'Okay,' he says as he goes and makes space to sit on the low seating.

'Would you like to eat something?' I ask. I am really hungry.

Eating is always the first thing I do when I come back home from work.

'No, it's okay,' he shakes his head.

'Are you sure?' I ask.

'Yeah, it's okay,' he nods.

'Are you sure? Because I am going to make Maggi,' I say.

'Okay.'

'Okay you'll have Maggi, or okay you won't?'

'Okay, I'll have some,' he says looking down at the floor.

'Okay, will just get it,' I say, smiling and go to the kitchen.

The water starts to boil and I empty the tastemaker sachet into the pan. That's how I like it. I always mix the tastemaker in the water before putting the noodles into it. Don't like the lumps of the masala in my Maggi. As I stir the boiling water to dissolve the tastemaker, I hear a guitar playing in the living room. It sounds something like 'Estella's Theme' from *Great Expectations* and is actually quite divine. The music rises and falls like the waves of the sea, almost transporting me to another world. I stand in the kitchen impatiently, waiting for the Maggi to be done. When it's done, I quickly empty the pan into a bowl, throw in two forks, pick up two plates from the dish rack and dash to the living room.

'You know how to play the guitar?'

Pranav stops playing and slowly puts the guitar down. 'I am sorry, I should have asked you before …' he trails into silence. He is behaving totally differently. It's unbelievable to see him so mild-mannered—it's unreal.

'No, no. It's okay. And that was good. Please, go on,' I encourage, pushing the guitar back in his hands. 'Play.'

People always underestimate the value of art in life. Art is all about soul and the metaphysical mojo that actually makes us the higher life form on this planet.

'Did you compose this tune yourself?' I ask him.

'Yes. I have composed a few more too if you would like to hear them.'

'Oh, I would love to!'

He smiles; he appears to have totally transformed. He is actually behaving like a nice person. Now I get why he has such a great fan following in college. He pulls out a notebook from his bag and opens it. I look closely, it's a music book. He knows how to write music notes? This is quite something! I'm impressed; even I don't know how to write music.

He starts playing another tune. It's as great as the previous one. I am almost lost in the tune and am staring in the air with unseeing eyes when he finishes playing and looks at me wide-eyed, waiting for me to comment.

'If you can compose music…' I finally speak, 'then why can't you make a painting?' I am remembering the bad painting he had submitted last week. It looked like a lame, half-hearted attempt of a sixth-class student for an art class.

He does not say anything and looks back at me blankly. He has no idea what I am trying to explain. He has no clue about the *universal laws of composition*.

'See,' I look deep into his eyes like a psychologist looks at his patient when he is about to hypnotize him and say, 'Unity, harmony, transition, balance and contrast—all these are the principles that we use to create music. And these are the same principles one would use to make paintings too.'

He looks back at me. He hasn't really understood anything.

'When you bring lines together, when you choose colours, when you choose forms to create a composition, you make your decisions using all these ideas for the kind of mood you want to create with your painting, the kind of expressions, the kind of feelings you want your audience to experience!'

He is still looking at me. Maybe he is getting it now.

'It's just like your music, only it's not audible. You can even transform your tunes and music into paintings.' Okay, I am starting to make no sense now. Music won't be music (in the literal sense, though many world renowned architects have called architecture 'music frozen in time', but still) if you can't hear it. I must shut up now.

I see him thinking hard, looking at the floor. This is good. *This is good!* I have initiated a reaction. I must let it roll. I must leave very silently without disturbing the energies in the room. I start stepping back without making any sound as Pranav pulls a sheet of paper from the pile of waste paper by his side and starts to sketch something.

Magic, this is magic! Faculty *does* have transforming magical abilities for their students. Just then my foot hits something on the floor and I topple over the centre table and fall. My hand plunges into the bowl of hot Maggi and I yelp in agony and pull my hand back. I land on the floor and the bowl lands next to me with a loud crash, upside down.

Pranav instantly looks up and gets up to help me.

'It's okay, it's okay,' I say as I gain balance and get up. 'You carry on. I just…' I say looking around, 'I will just clean this and … get some more Maggi.'

He steps back, sits down and picks up the paper again.

Thank god, *thank god*!

~

Things are going quite well at college. I have suddenly become Ranova's favourite teacher. And now that I think about it, maybe that was the secret behind Pranav's sudden change in behaviour as well. And it's not only the kids from my class who are coming for suggestions to me now. Kids from all batches come to me all the time—when I am having lunch, when I am preparing lectures, when I am in the library. They even come to me when I am taking classes for other students.

Another submission is due today. The kids were to turn in a paper on an artist of their choice and interpret and analyze his or her work as per their own understanding. I enter the classroom and sit on the table in my signature style.

'So, are we ready with the submission?'

'Yes, sir!' they say in unison.

'All right, please submit then,' I say, smiling.

All of them crowd around me and put their papers on my table. One student is looking at my ear and is not moving. What is he looking at? I am sure there is no ear wax oozing out. I cleaned them thoroughly after I took a bath in the morning. I touch my ear to check if everything is all right and then he speaks up sounding really disgusted, 'Sir, you have got hair growing out of your ear.' He pauses for a second or so, squints his eyes and says, 'You have bushy hair growing out of your nose too. Dude, you are *old*.'

Okay, this is *infuriating*. These kids are the most irritating, rude and ill-cultured lot ever. I want to chop off this kid's nose, drown him in acid and set him on fire! I look at him with rage in my eyes but he stares back with no sense of shame or regret whatsoever!

With a strict stare and a firm voice I say, 'I am going to scoop your eyes out, stuff your eye sockets with salt, pour kerosene in them, set them on fire and feed your eyeballs to the crows!'

Again, this is not even remotely close to what I could ever do but I say it with such conviction that the boy looks stunned and steps back. Within seconds, all the students move away and settle down on their seats.

I know I am watching too much of *True Blood* on TV these days and am getting influenced. I should not be talking to the students like this but then they should not be talking to me this way either.

They sit silently as I start going through their papers. What I see enrages me even more. None of them has tried to analyze anything or tried to put down their own thoughts on paper. All of them have copied material from Wikipedia. One after another ... all the papers read the same. My blood is boiling and I want to eat them all alive.

Picking up the bundle of papers, I say, 'This. Is. Not. Acceptable.' I walk right out of the class.

And walk straight into the dean's office. Jabba is sprawled on his chair as usual and licking a lollypop. His eyes are glued to a copy of *Fifty Shades Darker*. I stand in front of him and say, 'Sir.'

He is startled and instantly throws the book on the shelf behind him.

'Rohit! Come, come sit.'

I sit down and say, 'Sir, there is problem.' I keep the bundle of papers the kids have just submitted in front of him.

'Yes, yes. Tell me, tell.'

'Sir, I gave the second year students an assignment to write and they all copied it from Wikipedia.'

'Morons, they are *morons*!' he says as he starts chewing the lollypop he was licking. 'I know each and every one of them. I know them inside out. They sit here in my office and talk to me for hours. They are hardened criminals all of them, *hardened*. But I know how to control them, how to handle them. They are all my *puppets*!'

I sit there and again don't know how to react. Yes, what they have done is unacceptable, but criminals? *Hardened?* Don't know about that.

'They are all *animals*! They should be stripped naked and BEATEN!!' he says, staring at me with his eyes looking like saucers.

'And that's not all, sir, they keep misbehaving most of the time too,' I say. I know he is totally overreacting but I have to give vent to my frustration.

'Hardened! *Hardened!!*' he repeats. 'Next time, they turn in a submission likes this or misbehave with you, bring them to me, bring them all to me, *naked*.'

I sit dumbstruck again. This guy is totally demented. He really has some serious issues. 'And sorry, yaar. Sorry, they misbehaved,' he says as he shakes his head.

'It's okay, sir,' I say blankly.

'Sorry, yaar.'

19

And the gates open NOW—Karun

This is it! This is where it all starts. This day is going to go down in history as the day the greatest Indian author of all time signed the contract for his first book. I am sitting in Dash Publishers office and waiting for the owner of the firm, Mr D.K. Dé. If you really ask me, this place doesn't even come close to how I imagined it. India's hottest publisher at the moment, a person who has created history ... I thought he would have an impressive office. The place looks like a house filled with office furniture.

Mr D.K. Dé opens the door and enters the room.

I stand up.

'Hello, Karun, how are you?' he says.

'I am good, sir. How are you?'

'Please sit down,' he says as he sits on his big chair behind the table.

I smile and sit.

'I read your manuscript. It was interesting. I think we just need to make some minor changes and it should be ready for the press,' he says looking at me.

'Thank you, sir. That is great to know,' I smile.

'I think you should just add one or two sex scenes in the book. And use some other hot topics that are grabbing everyone's attention these days. I was reading in the newspaper the other day, homosexuality is a hot topic. Gays are coming out and there is something or the other about them in the news every day. Why don't you put a few jokes about gays in your book?' he asks.

'Yes, sir, we discussed this before also. I can sure give that a shot, sir.' He is insisting on the same idea. But it's okay. Anything to get my first book published man!

He smiles and says, 'It's good to have young, bright people like you as authors. The nation needs you; the nation needs to hear what young people like you have to say.'

'Thank you, sir.' He is a nice man. This is great.

'And do mail me a recent picture of yours when you go back, preferably in some natural surroundings. We maintain a record of all our authors who publish with us.

'Sure, sir.'

He takes a deep breath with his eyes fixed on me. After a few seconds or so he says, 'Establishing this publishing house was not easy. I have worked very hard.'

'I am sure, sir.'

'At times bad things happen only to push you to do bigger things in life. When I left Bang Bang Publishers, everyone told me that I was committing the biggest mistake of my life and should think again about leaving the company. But I was determined, determined to leave it and never to go back. *Chod aye hum wo galian …*' he smiles as he refers to an old song. 'And I had the most terrible start. I started with very few titles, mostly translations and classics. And they didn't sell, they didn't move in the market at all.'

He is a self-made man, he's seen the hardships of life.

'And then I published the first chicklet called *Nothing Here For Me, Sir*. That was the book that took the market by storm. It created publishing history. It sold so well that it gave competition to the highest selling author in India, Chirag Barot who published with Bang Bang. And then there was no looking back.'

Okay, he means chick-lit and not chicklet. And Bang Bang is the oldest publishing house in India. It's even older than independent India and this man sitting in front of me used to work with them, *smooth*!

'You must have been there when Chirag Barot's first book *5 Point 5 One* was launched by Bang Bang?' I ask. This is an inside story man! I am getting to know things that nobody else does.

He looks at me, smiles and nods.

'Wow!'

'And I was the one who established the title and sold it the way it did,' he says with his eyes fixed on me. 'Some people say that the first draft of his book was really bad.' He continues, 'And it was rewritten by one of his English teachers and he then sent it to the publishers. That is why his other books are so different from his first book.'

'Hmm … makes sense. Because I have read his other books and they are really terrible,' I say.

He only smiles and looks back at me.

I smile back.

'And today, our yearly collective sales are higher than Bang Bang's,' he says.

'That is really great to know sir.'

He smiles and says, 'God has his ways of showing you ups and downs in life. But everyone's fate is written. One should just keep doing one's work, everything else is destiny.'

He takes a cigarette out of his pocket and lights it up when I catch a glimpse of small circular burn marks on his hand. He notices me observing these marks and says, 'When the first few titles did not sell, I went into serious depression. I lost all hope and could not see any way out. I wanted to end things. I started getting suicidal thoughts. These marks are from that time.' He runs his fingers over the burn marks and says, 'I used to stub cigarettes on my skin. For some reason, pain had started giving me pleasure. But look at things now. I am the happiest person I know!'

I am at a loss for words. Interesting story and a strong person this Mr D.K. Dé is. But right now the only thing running through my mind is that I have to become the highest-selling author in his publishing house. The sales of *my* books need to outrun the yearly collective sales of Bang Bang Publishers. Chirag Barot needs to become history soon. My books need to sell more than his and I have to make that happen by all means.

'Let's go ahead with it then, let's sign the contract,' he says.

20

He feels like punching his publisher in the eye, again—Rohit

It was quite a day! I really wonder what these kids have on their minds. I mean what is their plan after all? All of them are well above eighteen. They are all adults and have the legal right to vote, they have the power to shape the nation for god's sake! This is seriously crazy. They don't even have the brains to shape their own life! They just don't believe in working. All they want to do is copy-paste and that's it. Thankfully, Pranav is working today. We had come back around five. He slept for an hour and has been working since. It's nine now. I am sitting on the couch in the living room and trying to watch television but nothing good is on. MTV is showing a re-run of some *Roadies* season in which some boys are tied to poles spread-eagled and will be hit in the balls if the girls don't give the right answer or something like that. Channel V is showing *Dare to Date*, another super disgusting show. I seriously wonder where the world is heading as I switch the television off and rest my head back on the sofa and close my eyes. I relax in the soothing silence of the room.

Just then I am startled as my phone starts to ring. The ringtone, Bon Jovi's 'It's My Life', violently echoes in the room, shattering the peaceful atmosphere. I jump for the phone and take the call.

It's Meetali, Nisha's journalist friend whom I had requested to review my next book.

'Hey!' I say cheerfully

'Hi,' she replies.

'How are you?' I ask.

'Good, how are you?'

'Good, I am good, yeah,' I say.

'So, how's your new book doing?'

'It's still to hit the market actually,' I say smiling, making sure my smile reflects in my voice.

'Yeah. You know, if you didn't want me to review your book, you should have told me straight, instead of playing such games.'

'What games?'

'I saw the book in the market today, Rohit.'

What the hell? Is the book out already? Did my publisher release the book without informing me?

'Hey, no, I didn't know the book was out. I emailed my publisher just three days ago and he said he would let me know as soon as the book reaches him.'

'Yeah … anyway, best of luck for your book. Bye,' she hangs up.

No! NNNOOOOOOOOO! It's the greatest epic NO

that my mind has ever screamed. (It's even more intense than Luke Skywalker's famous NO in *Star Wars*.) Things could not have gone worse; *things could not have gone worse than this*! I am going to kill my publisher! Why is he doing this to me? What does he have against me? He has completely butchered my plans for the promotions of my next book.

I am so annoyed I want to break everything around me. I want to burn the whole world down.

'Sir-ji,' I hear.

'What?' I yell as I turn to see Pranav peeping from behind the door. He is looking at me curiously.

'What's for dinner? I am hungry.'

I see a childish innocence in him as he speaks. 'Eggplant and potatoes,' I say flatly.

He stands there looking at me for about half a minute, hesitating to say something and finally speaks up. 'I don't want to eat eggplant. Can we please go out to eat today?' he says like a four-year-old. I am still really irritated but just don't have the heart to say no.

'Okay,' I respond and hope that going out will improve my mood.

21

The sexier and stronger 'sexy beast' becomes more mysterious—Jeet

After Lucknow, our destination is Goa. Her name is Neeti, by the way—the girl I met on the train and am travelling with now. Although we have not had any major action between us (if you know what I mean) it is still fun having her around. We are staying at a rather nice hotel called the Silver Sands and my room has the most enticing view of the beach. The sand almost seems to be silver. I had my book event yesterday and it went quite well. I had planned to surprise Neeti with my fame and popularity yesterday. But the whole thing turned out in such a way that I was the one who ended up surprised. I told her that I wanted to visit a bookstore and asked if she would like to come along. She agreed and was suitably astonished when we reached the bookshop.

'What is all this?' she asked looking at the standees, porters and piles of my book in the bookstore. 'Oh my god, you are a writer!! Oh my god, you are a *big* writer!! I had no idea.

My god, this is something I could have never imagined!' she said amazed. Her reaction was totally out of character (such overacting). But I always get a kick out of it when people are overwhelmed by my fame and profile. Acting humble and pretending to be embarrassed, I said, looking at the floor, 'I guess I am … what do you say.'

She burst out laughing, 'I am sorry… but I really can't pretend anymore. Oh my god, that look on your face.'

I looked at her questioningly.

'I am sorry but I have known that you are Jeet Obiroi, the author of that famous book, all along!'

And that was when I was actually embarrassed.

'I was just playing this game with you.'

'What game?' I asked.

'You will know in time,' she said with a smile.

I stood there confused, looking at her. Did that mean that everything she had told me was a lie as well? Was she not getting married? Because if that was so, then there was not much of a chance that I … you know. It's a fact that many girls want to try out a different guy just before they get married. There are studies on that.

'So everything you told me was a lie? You are not getting married?' I asked

She laughed again and said, 'What I told you about me was true. I am not a liar like that.'

I was relieved and hopeful again. After that, all through my event she kept smiling at me, sitting in the front row, boosting my confidence.

We are staying in the same hotel but she has insisted on

taking different rooms. We had planned to be in Goa for three days. This is our last evening, our last walk on the beach.

She told me she would meet me at the beach at 6.30 and it's already 6.25. I must push out now. I reach the beach and see her standing against the sun that is nearing the horizon. She is looking ravishing. She is talking to someone on the phone and is wearing a loose blue spaghetti top with a floral pattern and a dark blue sarong. The golden sunlight of dusk is giving her smooth shoulders a soothing glow. She is standing at the edge of the water where tiny waves are coming and kissing her ankles, tickling her feet and leaving her smiling as they recede into a sea that seems to be singing a song of joy.

'Hi,' I say.

She turns around, looks at me and says cheerfully, 'Hey.' She speaks into the phone and says, 'I will call you back.' And disconnects the call.

'Beautiful sunset, isn't it?'

'Yes, it is,' she says with a peaceful smile. The evening breeze is softly playing with her curly hair and gently caressing my bare chest.

Looking at me, she says after a few seconds, 'I always wonder how you guys manage it. I wonder how such loose jeans which sit way below your waist and always threaten to fall never actually fall.'

I look at my low-waist jeans and then at her. I am wearing only a pair of jeans on my grey jockeys for a reason—there is no better place to flaunt your body than on a beach in Goa.

'I don't know about the rest but I have an active system in place to hold it up,' I say with a cocky smile.

She turns away and says, 'Mind a walk?'

'Not at all!' I say.

'So, a big shot author, huh? I see very good promotions for your book everywhere. How do you manage all this?'

'It's not all that tough. These days all one needs to do is hire a good PR agency and be active with the follow-ups. Things work quite smoothly this way.'

She smiles, 'Interesting! Sounds like being famous is a game of money more than anything else.' I listen to her saying that and I feel anxious. Was it just pure luck that gave me all I have today and brought me here?

It feels like just yesterday when I was discussing the possibilities of the book with Karishma, my best friend in college. I might keep trying to convince myself that I am getting all the recognition because I was destined for it, but I can never deny that it happened all because of her. I still clearly remember that afternoon when we were at her place and were discussing the possible ways to promote the book at a national level. Her father ran a well-known PR firm and there was no other person who could have guided us better.

Funny how relationships change and how friends drift apart. Karishma's father made me someone all right but things have changed so much. Back in college, Karishma and I were inseparable. People used to bet that we would end up getting married, we were that compatible. But it was so hard staying in touch after college. There were regular phone calls and emails for a few months in the beginning. But now I don't even know if she is working with the same firm she was when we spoke six months ago or if she has taken up a new job.

And for that matter, even which city she is in.

I turn and look at Neeti to bring myself back to reality. I look at her beautiful, big eyes that seem to be silent and yet so active, the curve of her neck and defined collar bone, her smooth skin and the teasing glimpse of her cleavage.

'You know something?' I ask looking at her.

She looks up at me.

'They say I am a very good kisser.'

She laughs, 'Really? I have my doubts!'

'Are you challenging me?' I say flexing my triceps and then my abs.

'So, this is how you make advances. Interesting. Yes, I would like to see how good a kisser you are. But don't let that put any ideas in your mind. I was a stage actor back in college. And actors, as you know, are very free with their bodies. A kiss won't mean anything to me.'

She is not even done speaking when I gently put my hands on her bare shoulders and lightly touch my lips to hers. She kisses me back and we stand there—a long, warm kiss. Finally she pulls back. I stand there with my heart racing for a few seconds. She is an amazing kisser! I want to kiss her again. I move towards her soft lips but she puts her hand on my chest, pushes me back and does not move her hand. She feels my heart beating. Lightly brushing the hair on my chest, she runs her hand down my chest, to my abs and then moves it away. She looks into my eyes, turns and starts walking. I follow her and ask, 'So, how was it?'

She keeps walking, looks me, smiles and says, 'I think I have had better.'

22

**Can he ever stand strong? Can he ever stand strong
and question his publisher?—Rohit**

This is crazy! I just can't keep sitting quietly about this. It's *my*
book and *I* had the first right to know when it hit the market.
I am fuming as I dial my publisher's number. I am going to fire
him today. And if he does not take my call today, I swear I am
going hire a bounty hunter—the best there is in the business.

After eight rings, he takes the call.

'Hellow!'

'Hello, sir, how are you?' Damn it, *damn it*! This is not the
tone I want to use. This is not the tone!!!

'Hello, Rohit, how are you?'

'Good, sir, how are you?' Fuck! *Fuck!*

'I was trying your phone yesterday,' he says, 'but I could
not get through. And then there were such heavy clouds in
the sky and it became so dark and started raining so hard that
I thought I would call tomorrow. But before I could call, you
called. See how thoughts travel … telepathy, huh?'

What trash, what trash is he talking? 'Actually, sir, I wanted to know if my second book has come from the printer yet,' I say, finally achieving the tone I want to use with him.

'Yes, yes. That is what I wanted to tell you yesterday.'

'Okay, and it's reached the bookstores also?'

'Yes, yes, all the major bookstores!'

I am furious now. He has got some nerve to say that.

'Also, sir, I wanted to know what impression my first book is running in right now.'

'Yes, yes, I will check and let you know,' he says, almost as if he is singing a song.

'Also, sir, if you could send me the details of the sale figures for my first book. I want to see those.'

'Oh! Sale figures, oh … okay.'

'And, sir, I was also thinking that with the release of my second book, the sales of my first book should also revive. We must try to cash in on the market. We must supply the first book in good quantity and we should also increase the print run for the book.'

'Pardon?'

I know he has heard every word and is just pretending. I repeat. There is silence at his end, then, 'I will look into that.'

I want to shoot him. I want to put a bullet in his head. Why can't he just do what I'm asking him to? It's plain and simple logic!

'Sir, I think this is really necessary and we need to do this.'

'Okay, okay we won't put this on paper but it will be our mutual understanding that from this month onwards we increase the print run.'

'Thank you.'

'Okay, Rohit!'

'Yes, sir.'

'Bye!'

'Bye!'

Huh! Stupid asshole! What was he thinking?

~

I am in the HOD's office once again. These authority people, they keep summoning the new recruits all the time. She is on the phone and has asked me to wait for a bit. From the looks of it, she is talking to some hotshot higher authority. After a minute or so, she hangs up and looks at me.

'So, how is it going?'

'Going cool, ma'am,' I say, totally unsure of what she means.

'Pranav is not much trouble. You just need to give him the right amount of attention and care he craves.'

'Yeah, he is a totally different kid at home. Nothing like what he is like in college. He is also working regularly on his project now and does not misbehave in my class either. I don't know about the other classes though.'

'The reports are not that severe from the other teachers now,' she says, going through the pile of papers on her table.

'That is very good news, then,' I smile.

'You know, Rohit, when I started teaching. I was given the final year to teach as my first job assignment. When I was told about it, my hands would not stop shaking. You know how students are? Nasty is an understatement for final year students.

But I was always the person who derived a thrill out of facing challenges. I was the girl who wanted to ride an Enfield if you want to categorize me. So I went ahead with it. And before I went on to deliver my first class, my HOD told me that the faculty has magic. They can turn around a student's life like no one else in the world. But the problem is that very few people are aware of this fact, very few people believe it. That time, when I heard him, I didn't know what he was saying. But today I realize how true he was. Teachers influence their students in ways in which even their parents can't.'

She says it with such strong conviction that I am forced to think about it. It sounds all good and everything, like teachers with magic in the Harry Potter books. I don't know how true it is though.

23

**Oh! That sweet love! That sweet and mushy
love!—Karun**

My friends have done exactly what I expected them to do.
The news that I have signed the contract for my debut novel
with Dash Publishers has spread like wildfire. It's lunch right
now and they have invited Lovanya and her friends to eat with
them (again). After I join them, they are going to do exactly
as I have instructed them to.

I hold the brown paper bag close to my chest and walk with
my heart pounding. I have never felt it beating so hard. I can
actually hear the *lubb dubb* sound in my thoracic cavity, which
our biology teacher always tried to explain to us.

I spot Lovanya and my friends sitting on the lawn. I take
a deep breath and walk towards them.

'Hello,' I say when I reach them.

'Hey!' they all say together.

I look at Lovanya and she smiles. I nod. It is amazing how
she manages to look so ravishing in the same school uniform

every day. For a few seconds I can't take my eyes off her. Her skin is glowing in the sunlight. I look at her face and can't stop admiring it. Her clear jaw line that ends behind a soft and tender earlobe makes me want to look at it forever. Her supple cheeks make me want to kiss them.

'So, what's up?' I ask looking at Ishan, giving him the cue.

'Nothing, we were just sitting, just like that,' he says. He looks at me and then says suddenly, 'Hey, who wants to have an ice cream?'

'I do!' Gaurav jumps up instantly.

'Great! Let's go and have some,' he says as all of them get up. Lovanya is about to stand up when Ishan says, 'Hey, you stay here, we will get one for you. Which ice cream do you want to have?'

'Orange bar,' she says with an awkward expression as she settles down again.

'Orange bar it is,' Ishan nods and all of them go, leaving me and Lovanya alone.

I go and sit next to her.

'So, signed a contract for your novel, huh? Good job, congratulations,' she says.

'Thank you.' I smile.

Silence.

I can't keep sitting here dumbly, looking at the grass. I have to do what I came here for.

My heart starts beating even faster and I muster all my courage and say, 'I ... got something for you.'

'What?' she asks and I suddenly lose my voice. Okay, this does not suit me. I have just signed a contract with one of the ace publishers of the country. And I am going to be the highest-selling author in India soon, there is no way I am going to chicken out of this.

'I got a present for you,' I speak up as I pull the gift out of the brown paper bag. It's wrapped in beautiful white wrapping paper that has small red hearts on it. I bought it from an Archies Gallery. I have also tied a thin red satin ribbon that meets in a bow knot right at the geometrical centre of the rectangular face of the packet.

'You shouldn't have, gifts make me uncomfortable. And moreover, *you* have signed a contract for your book; we all should be giving *you* a present.'

'Please don't say no. Please accept this, it would mean a lot to me,' I say as I look into her eyes.

She smiles. 'What is it?' she asks as she takes the gift from my hands.

'Open it,' I smile.

She unties the ribbon, letting it fall in her lap, and removes the wrapping paper without ripping it. She smiles at what she sees and looks like an angel.

'Your book,' she says.

'Yes.' It took me over three hours last night to prepare the first copy of my book. It was a total of 209 pages. I had to cut the A4 papers into half as I did not have any A5 papers (which is close to the size of the book we get in the market. A set of A4 printouts bound together would have looked only stupid.) After that the real battle started; my printer just does not like me. It was paper jam after paper jam and endless system failures. It not only tested my patience but also made me cut more A4 sheets into halves. But anything for my love, my angel. I had the prints for my first novel, my story about how much I love Lovanya and what all I can do for her. The first thing I did after I came to school today was to rush to the tuck shop and give them the printouts for binding. I had to promise two 5-star chocolates to the boy who works there in return for binding the book on priority and having it ready by recess—the things we do for love.

She turns the cover page and reads what's written on the next page as she runs her fingers over it.

For the love of my life, my angel.

I have dedicated the book to her.

'I have written this book for you, my angel,' I say.

24

Those mind-wrecking, suicide-motivating hate mails!—Rohit

You there, yes, you, the author of that pathetic book, yes I am talking to you.

I read ur book (I mean I tried reading it), but it is one of the most boring books with passages taken from here and there. All of what you have said seems to be made up like a 3-4 year old writing his girlfriend's name on the desk. Pathetic! I am sure u r a talented boy in something else but not writing. No, I am not comparing you with someone like Bhetan Chagat. For example take Jeet Obiroi. That's what we all call writing a story and presenting it in a way that the audience feels connected. Anyways ... I have decided to give the book back to where I got it from and that too for free.

```
    Face it. It's worthless.
    Sorry to be harsh but that's the way I
felt when I read that thing.
    Someone who wants to show you a mirror,
    Abhishek
```

I sit stunned, staring at the screen of my laptop. Was my book that bad that it pushed someone to write such an angry mail? But no one forced this person to read this book, right? If he wasn't enjoying it, he could have quit reading it. Why send me such an abusive email? And does he even know the difference between a reader and an audience?

'What are you reading, sir-ji?' It's Pranav, his head popping in between me and the screen, almost hitting my nose.

I am too depressed to hide the mail. 'Nothing, it's just a hate mail.'

He reads the mail, laughs and says, 'Sir-ji, someone really hates you.'

'I guess.' This is bloody depressing.

'Sir-ji, lets go out and eat momos.'

By god! This kid is seriously crazy! I don't even know which crazy planet he is from.

~

We are going to the nearby market. This kid just won't rest. If I had said no, he would have started sulking. It was best to just go.

I am about to open the gate when he almost shouts, 'Sir-ji,

one minute!' He looks at the gate carefully. It's a metal gate about four feet high.

He takes a few steps back, runs to the gate, grabs the top bar firmly, leaps up, smoothly swinging both his legs over the gate. After landing on the other side of the gate, he turns around and says, 'Your turn.'

I stare back at him, gobsmacked. What is he expecting?

'If you fall, I'll catch you,' he says.

'Okay, so that is your plan. You want me to do that so that I crash and fall and break my arms or legs and you can happily do whatever you want as there would be no classes for you,' I say.

'Sir-ji, you never do anything fun,' he says as he walks on.

We are in the market now and the momos are quite yum.

'Sir-ji, can I ask you something?'

'No,' I reply plainly.

'Why do you write?' he asks without hesitation, as if my 'no' had no meaning. 'I mean … what makes you write? What compels you to do it?'

I stare back at him. He has asked me a sensible question for the first time and I must answer him (sensibly). This is the time to use the magic!

'It's an urge that comes from within, a craving to … write stories, to make people laugh, to … subtly teach them lessons for life.' I have his full attention.

'And how do you get the stories? How do you get the ideas?' he asks.

'They just come to me; they just hit me like a wave of energy,' I say as I think of Nisha. 'And, I feel that I conceive the stories because the world needs them. And god wants me to tell these stories to the world. For if he didn't want that, I wouldn't get the ideas. I feel that I am only following god's wishes and there is no way I am going to stop doing that, no matter how much my publisher cheats me. And that, I feel, is the purpose of my life,' I conclude.

He looks at me wide-eyed and then finally asks, 'Do I also have purpose?'

'Yes,' I say.

'What if I don't?'

'Not possible. If you didn't have a purpose, you wouldn't exist.'

There is silence for full thirty seconds as he looks at the ground and thinks about something. I pray that his thoughts are travelling in the right direction.

'You know, sir-ji, when you started teaching us, everyone thought that you were a strange teacher and they all made fun of you. But now everyone thinks that you are the best teacher in the whole college!'

'Hmm.' I don't know what to say, it's an awkward moment. I am not used to praise. But I smile.

'And that is why students from all years come to you for discussions,' he says.

'Hmm.'

25

Some people know how to flatter and reach everyone—Jeet

This tour for my book promotion is turning out to be a huge success. After the awesome event at the Red Book Store, Goa, we had another one at the Red Book Store, Mumbai, that went equally well. It was a good decision to have a tie-up with the Red Book Store chain. Not only are they a big name when it comes to bookstores, they also have a good relationship with the media. And for some reason, with Neeti by my side, I am getting extra attention at each event. I have a feeling it makes me look more important. Maybe people like you more when they see someone likes you already.

It's midnight and I have just come back after having dinner with Neeti. She is in her room three doors down the corridor. She is a very nice girl; it's a pity she is getting married. But I know for sure that I am going to sleep with her before this trip ends. I look at the clock on the wall and am reminded of the time. I must sleep now, it's going to be a long day tomorrow—

an early morning flight to Kolkata and a book event in the evening. I turn on my computer to quickly check any mail before calling it a day. There is one new message.

```
Hey Sir,
    This is Karun, your biggest fan on the
face of this earth—the one who met you at
your Delhi book event at the Red Book Store
last month? I said that I wanted to stay in
touch with you and you said that it would
be best if I mailed you. So here I am.
    Actually sir, I needed a little help from
you. I am working on my first novel and need
your guidance. I would be grateful if you
would give me your phone number so that I
could have a discussion with you.
    I hope that this mail reaches you and not
any of your assistants who may not pass my
message to you. And I hope you reply.
    Thank you,
    Your biggest fan
    Karun Mukharjee
```

I remember this kid from Delhi. He'd asked for my phone number earlier too. So he is writing a book, interesting … Maybe it would be a good idea to give him my number and have a discussion with him. Who knows what possibilities might emerge? He may agree to have me as co-author for his book if that guarantees that the book will be published.

26

He does not have the looks or the charm. Will he ever become a successful author?—Rohit

It's a wonderfully bright morning and I feel totally alive today. I walk to the living room and see the newspaper lying on the floor. The newspaper vendor has slipped it in from underneath the door. It lies there beautifully at an angle as it is touched by the golden morning light coming from the window to the left. I pick it up, put it on the table, get my tea from the kitchen and peacefully sit down to read the magazine section. It's the most interesting section of the newspaper, I always start with it.

I almost spurt my tea out and want to burn my eyes after what I see. It's a full-page spread on Jeet Obiroi's book launch. What they are saying in the article is mindlessly ridiculous!

The headline reads, THE SKETCH OF AN AUTHOR AS A CUTE GUY.

'The new face of popular Indian fiction has dimples to die for and 25,000 fans on Facebook!'

It is a long article, talking only about how good looking and popular the author is and saying nothing at all about his writing. The article also very boldly states that the author's good looks are a major reason for his books selling so well.

I am doomed! I am finished!! My writing career is over!!! I have zero good looks, negative sex appeal and a repulsive way of carrying myself. (That is way my students made fun of me when I started teaching them.) There is no way anyone is ever going want to read my books! I am *doomed*!

But this is not really news, these things have been in circulation on Facebook since like forever. Whenever this author put up a new picture of himself on his Timeline, it got 800 likes and 150 comments within five minutes. 'Oh cutee pie!!!', 'You are so cute, I love you!!!' is how most of the comments read. I remember talking to Nisha about it once. She thought it was insane. What would she have said today after reading this? I sit back and try to picture her talking.

'No intelligent person will pick up this author's book after reading this article,' she would have said. Yes, that is *so* true. I never pick up a book based on the author's picture. I would only want to know what the story is. Consider George R.R. Martin, for example. He is no good looker but I love his books. But wait a minute! My target readership consists of teenagers, and they *are* driven by looks. They live in a superficial world—short, sexy skirts and tight T-shirts!!! Oh no! I do need to panic.

I hear Nisha in my mind again. *Only people without brains pick up books like that and if I were in your place, I would not want those mindless people to read my books.*

Yes, that is right, I must not care for people like that, I must not.

'Sir-ji, good morning,' I hear Pranav as he comes out of his room.

'Morning,' I say.

'What are you reading?' he asks me.

'Nothing, just the newspaper.'

He comes over and takes a look.

'People buy books these days because the authors look cute,' I say simply stating the fact.

'That's not tough, you can look good too. You just need to get a good picture of yourself clicked,' he says casually.

Okay, he knows nothing. It is almost impossible to get a good picture of me. All my pictures can be classified into three categories:

a) The ones in which I look like a turtle.

b) The ones in which I look like a baboon.

c) The ones in which I look like a horse.

'Huh! As if that is a possibility,' I sigh.

He looks at me as if he has heard what was just going on in my mind.

'Sir-ji, do you realize you have issues with yourself?' he asks, looking at me.

'Do you realize you are getting late for college?' I say flatly, without looking at him.

~

I am dead tired and don't want to work today. My brain is feeling numb and I just can't write anything. It was such a long day at college. I am going to take this evening off. Pranav is working in his room and that is good—he won't come to disturb me. Each time I sit down to watch something on TV, he has to watch *Roadies*. It is such a disgusting show but he *has* to watch it.

I switch channels when I see *Breakfast at Tiffany's* is on at one.

'The name is Cat,' Audrey says as her big round eyes look more beautiful than ever. God! She is so beautiful. Each time I look at her I am reminded of Nisha. But no, I won't call her. Why should *I* always call her? She should call now, I am not going to call. Irritated, I turn the TV off. But there is no silence. Pranav has got music on in his room 'and I'm gonna miss you like a child misses a blanket...' goes the song. God! I want to talk to her. I want to talk to her *now*!!

I pick up the phone and dial her number. I am sure she is dying to talk to me too. She is going to say she missed me and she loves me as soon as she picks up the phone. We are so used to each other!

'Hello,' she says.

'Hey! How are you?'

'Good. Hey, we are in the middle of a movie. I'll call you back,' she says.

'Oh! Okay, okay, bye.' I say.

'Bye,' she hangs up.

This is not done! This is just not done. I call her after a whole week and she says she will call back?

I furiously punch a message. I am punching on my touch screen phone so hard that it might just break.

IF YOU WANT THIS REALTIONSHIP TO CONTINUE,
U HAVE TO CALL ME NOW.

After a minute my phone rings.

'Hello,' she says.

'Do you realize we have not spoken for over a week?'

'Yes,' she says plainly.

'Do you realize ... it's like not being a part of each other's life anymore?'

'No, it's not, we are just busy.'

'Yes, it is. There is so much that has happened with me here. You have no idea that I have a student staying with me at my place here and you have no idea how terribly my career is crashing right now.'

'Rohit, why does it always have to be about you and only you? Why can't you ever think about anyone else? Do you have any idea what is going on in *my* life right now? Okay, just tell me what is wrong with your life so that I can give you a quick pep-talk and let's just hang up.' She sounds angry. This is completely unlike her—she is never angry.

'What do you mean?' I ask.

'I want you to get to the point, Rohit. You always want to talk whenever you face a problem. And *that* is when you want to talk to me. I am nothing but a problem solver for you. So why don't you just tell me what your problem is right now. What do you need? I'll give you a solution. Let's just do that and end this conversation.' She is on fire.

'How ... how dare you! How dare you accuse me of that?'

'How dare *you*, Rohit! You know how important the assignment is for me. And when I said that I was busy and would call you later you send me a threatening message like this? How dare *you*?'

'This is done; it can't go on like this.' I am serious.

'I know, it can't. You just pull me down. I will never be able to grow if you are around,' she says brutally.

'I guess there is no point in being together then.'

'Yes,' she says and my heart burns like it has never burnt before. I disconnect the call. I don't even say bye.

Right after the call, I open the contacts list in my phone and delete her number. Huh! Forgot you!

27

As someone is breaking up with his girlfriend and cursing himself for having a shoddy writing career, someone is becoming really popular (locally)—Karun

Who says that one needs to be slow and steady to be successful? The days of the tortoise are gone. It's the cyber age now and everything happens as quickly as the click of a button. And my Facebook profile is testimony to the fact. I have logged on after eight hours and there are 128 new friend requests! The whole school has gone nuts. Everyone wants to be my friend. Even kids from the third standard are sending me requests. I check my blog where I had uploaded the first chapter from my novel yesterday, and it has already got 546 hits. Girls from every class have commented on it with hearts, kisses and what not. They love it: 'It's the cutest love story I have ever read and just can't wait to read the rest of the story.' I am hot property now, man! I am the most popular boy in the school, by all means, I am! Boy, this is crazy. *And I love it!*

28

**Oh my God! This is why he gets those nightmares!
This is his secret!—Jeet**

The media has covered the Kolkata event quite well. The *Calcutta Post* has a full page feature on the front page of its magazine section. The article has a big picture of me with Neeti sitting next to me as part of the panel. In the picture, I am speaking and she is looking at me and has a naughty smile on her face. This time the feature has a little bit of spice too. Apart from the other things, it says,

> Rumour has it that bestselling author Jeet Obiroi is 'seeing' someone these days as he has been 'seen' with someone a lot lately. The 'mystery girl', as some are calling her, attends all his events religiously and was actually a part of the discussion panel for this event. Maybe the hot author has decided to say goodbye to singlehood. And they are together not just during the events. Some eyes claim to have seen them having 'romantic sunset walks' along Marine Drive in Mumbai and some beaches in Goa …

Neeti and I are at the hotel café waiting for our breakfast.

'These journalists really know how to cook up stories, don't they?' I say passing the newspaper to her.

She takes a few seconds to run through the lines, smiles and says, 'They only cook up stories about famous people, about the people they are interested in.'

I look at her and smile. What is really going on in her mind? Does she like me? What do I mean to her? Does she only want to have a one-night stand with me; if given a choice, would she actually choose me over the person who has been *arranged* for her?

She looks at me, squints and frowns. 'What's wrong with you? Why are you looking at me like that?'

'Nothing, just like that … nothing.'

'Oh my god!' she says, wide-eyed.

'What?'

'Oh my god, you are getting ideas!'

'What ideas?'

'*Love* ideas!'

'*No!*

'Yes! Reading that article. Smiling. Looking at me like that. God! You are definitely getting ideas!'

'No, I am not!' Am I going red in the face? My cheeks feel warm.

'Okay, I think it's time for me to tell you why I am here with you and why I have been tagging along with you.'

I gulp. What does she mean? Is she here because she knows my secret? Is she a journalist who has come to unmask me in front of everyone? Is she going to write a nasty newspaper article about me? Is she the journalist I saw in my dream? I look at her curly hair and can almost see the face of the journalist I saw in my dream. God! How could I be so foolish? How could I not have realized this before?

'That I'm getting married in two months is not the only reason why I came with you on this trip. It's going to sound very cheap and I really don't know how to put it but ...' she trails into silence.

Okay, so she just wants some crazy sex with me. That's okay. She can be open about it. We live in the twenty-first century—it's totally fine.

'I have been working on a novel.' She takes a deep breath and says, 'I have been working on it for over a year now and I'm almost done with my manuscript. I have sent the proposal to many publishers but none of them have shown interest.'

I do not say anything as I listen to her.

'Even Dash publishers, the king of popular fiction right now, did not accept it. In fact, they didn't even reply. I mailed them my proposal some five times and they did not even acknowledge that they had received my mails.'

She looks at me and says, 'I was just hoping to get some contacts from you that would help me get published. And if that doesn't not work, I was going to offer to have you as co-author of my book as that would not only help the book get published but also help sales.'

I listen to her, paralyzed. And clearly recall the day my first book came to me.

I had gone over to Karishma's house that afternoon. Her mother had made matar-paneer and rice and had invited me over for lunch. She knew how much I loved matar-paneer. It was a hot summer afternoon and searing winds were rolling dry leaves on the street outside. I went to Karishma's room and knocked on the door. She was reading a novel, and a blue file was lying next to her.

'What are you doing?' I had asked her most lamely.

'Nothing,' she said, keeping her book aside.

'What is this?' I asked, opening the blue file kept by her side.

'Nothing, just some stupid thing I wrote before I joined college,' she said casually.

I read a few lines and found the language quite crisp and quirky.

'Looks good. Is it like a novel?'

'Yes, you can say that. But it's really trashy.'

I read a few lines and the writing really grabbed my attention. It was a conversation between a guy and a girl who had met each other for the first time on a blind date that their friends had set up for them.

'I think it's quite nice. Have you finished writing the whole story?'

'Yes, but believe me, it's really terrible.'

'Oh come on, this is really cool. Have you ever thought of getting it published?'

'This piece of trash? No way! And who's going to publish it anyway? No one would be that crazy. No publisher would want to burn their money.'

'I think you are being stupid by not trying to get it published.'

'Jeet, if I ever want to get published, it won't be with this book. This is trashy … pulp fiction stuff. If I ever want to get published, it will be with something more serious, something more meaningful.'

'But believe me, this is really cool. It's really funny,' I said laughing, reading a few lines from the manuscript.

'There is no way I am going to get it published under my name. If this gets published, it will either get published anonymously or under a pen name.'

I continued to read.

'Or, if you want, you can get it published under your name.'

I had looked up from the manuscript.

That was the beginning of it all.

29

**Because he knows what he wants, because he knows
where he is going—Karun**

School is such a waste of time. If only we didn't need all these
certificates and degrees. I come to school every day and learn
nothing new. I know more than my teachers. They are all
useless—most of all, our English teacher. It's the English class
again and I am stuck. Lovanya is absent today and I can't even
write poems and songs and pass on to her. I don't know how
to kill the time. I have already made seven different cartoons
of the Dirty Dragon from all possible angles and can't think
of any more ways to draw him.

I am sitting and pretending to listen to the Dragon when
someone pokes me in the back. I am smooth with things; I do
not jump or react. I only look back to see who it is, making sure
the Dragon does not notice me. I turn back and see Devika. She
smiles when I look at her and passes me a folded chit. Who is
Devika? If Lovanya is the prettiest girl in school, then Devika is the
hottest—it's as simple as that. I turn around and unfold the chit.

Meet me at the cycle stand after school;)

Interesting. I wonder what's on her mind.

'Karun, please meet me after class,' I suddenly hear the Dragon say. He has caught me completely off guard. Damn! Now he is going to bore me with one of his lectures about values and stuff. I so hate it when this happens—when he makes you sit in front of him and talks to you one on one, you can't even draw his cartoons (or do anything else for that matter). I just look at him and nod.

~

The period is over and it's recess. Everyone is moving out with their lunch boxes, smiling, laughing and excited and I have to meet the boring Dirty Dragon. He is sitting on a chair behind his table, gathering his papers and books and piling them up. I go and stand in front of him. He looks up and says, 'I know what I am going to say and and I also know that it's going to be a total waste on you, but what can I do? I can't stop myself from trying to help you become a better person … I am a teacher.'

I let out a sigh—there he goes again.

'I have known you for years now, Karun. It's not right, the way you look at the world. With such blind arrogance, you are *never going to gain anything, never going to learn anything*.'

What I hear only makes me smile.

'Never going to gain anything,' he says.

'You have known me for years, sir. I am not a kid anymore. I am a grown up and I know what I want from my life. And, as for gaining anything, I didn't tell you that I signed a contract for my first novel with a publisher last week. So it's not that easy to say who's gaining *anything* in this world and who's not,' I say as he looks back at me with a fixed stare. I know he has written a novel himself and has been struggling to find a publisher for the past four years. The whole school looks up to him as someone who has accomplished something great by completing a novel. But soon everyone is going to consider me even greater than him—not only have I finished a novel but I will also have successfully managed to get it published!

He keeps looking at me, speechless. I have shut him up; he has nothing to say to me. He is a loser and I have shown him the mirror. It's true: Those who can, do; those who can't, teach. There are so many people who fail to do anything in life and end up becoming teachers. And if you really ask me, this is why the Indian education system is in such a terrible state.

I am about to leave when he speaks up, 'There are two kinds of people in this world, Karun. The ones who worship art and knowledge, those who worship Saraswati Ma, and the ones who worship wealth, Lakshmi Ma. And if you ever plan to pursue anything that demands creativity, you cannot achieve anything without Saraswati Ma's blessings. And she blesses only the ones with a pure and good heart. Remember this if you ever want to achieve anything in life. Momentary gain and momentary success is different. It's easy to achieve and can come quick. But success for life is something else. It doesn't come that easily and is hard to achieve.' He looks at me for a while, picks up his books and papers and leaves.

For a minute his words ring in my ears—*she blesses only the ones who have a pure and a good heart*. And then I realize—it's all horse shit.

~

School is over for the day and I am excited. Devika has asked me to meet her at the cycle stand and I just can't wait to know what it is about. Bag slung on my shoulder, I walk to the stand and see her sitting lazily on the carrier of a cycle with one foot touching the ground and one foot in the air. She is looking sexy. There is no doubt about that. I walk up to her. 'Hi,' I smile.

She gets off the cycle, smiles and says, 'Hi.'

There is a moment of silence and I finally speak up, raising an eyebrow, 'So?'

She smiles again and says, 'So, the thing is that I am a very straightforward person and I say things directly.'

My mind starts to jump as soon as I hear that. I had always heard that girls find guys who write irresistible and sexy, but never thought it would happen to me so soon. I check her out—she has the perfect figure.

She lets out a sigh and throws her hands up in the air, 'Guys will always be guys! What you are thinking right now is not even close … So please don't start dreaming, stupid.'

Okay, now she has me confused. Why did she call me here after school? She knows that this becomes a deserted spot soon after the final bell rings and that we would be *alone* here.

'Control your wild thoughts and listen up. I know that you have signed a contract for your first novel and you will get published soon. And if you have any speck of ambition inside you, or any intelligence for that matter, you should start looking for a story for your next novel. This is where I come in. I have a really hot story in my mind that I want to write. But I know how hard it is to get published. So we co-author the book. I get published and you get your next story, it's win-win for both of us.'

I listen to her and think about what she just said. I look at her and contemplate and assess—she is smart, sharp, brutal, hot, straightforward, quick and a go-getter. She could be useful for my plan too.

'Okay,' I say as I run my thumb along the inside of the strap of my bag on my shoulder, 'but there is one thing that we need to do before we sign up for our book with the publisher.'

'What?'

'Throw all the other authors out of the publishing house and become the king and the queen of Dash Publishers.'

She looks at me with a devilish smile and says, 'I like that.'

30

He loves momos and he believes that his publisher is an A-hole—Rohit

It is no big deal at all that I have broken up with Nisha. We have been out of each other's life for the past month (almost) and I am already used to living without her. In fact, I think this is the best break up in history—you grow used to living without each other and then you break up. It's the best thing and everyone should break up like this. I am thinking all this as I walk to the dean's office. I wonder why Jabba has called me this time. I am sure he is going to ask me if the kids are behaving themselves and then shove a piece of chocolate in his mouth, smear it all over his face, shake his head and say, 'Sorry, yaar.' Or maybe he is going to congratulate me for doing a great job here. Pranav was saying that I am the students' favourite teacher. Moreover, students from all the batches have been coming to me to discuss their projects. I am sure I am doing things right. Maybe he wants to give me more classes to teach; I do have three hours less of work per week as compared to everybody else.

I open the door to Jabba's cluttered office and see him on his chair with a book in his hand. I can't see what book it is because he has covered it with a newspaper. But I have a feeling that it is *Fifty Shades Freed* (I'm almost certain) as his other hand is where it always is and I pretend that I don't see it.

'Yes, Rohit, please come,' he says as he sees me. 'Come, sit.'

I settle down as he puts the book he was reading on the table and gets up. As he does so, I catch a glimpse of his bulging belly and his belly button, and quickly look away, embarrassed. Poor thing, it's not his fault he is so fat. It is practically not possible to make the button and the buttonhole meet over the circumference of his paunch.

'Just give me a second,' he says as he turns and around and goes through some papers shabbily piled on the bookshelf behind his chair.

I take a quick peek at the book he was reading. Aha! I was right! It is *Fifty Shades Freed*. Ha ha ha!

He pulls out a sheet of paper, turns around and sits down.

'I monitored the performance of the students in your class and I must say I was *very* disappointed,' he says shaking his head. 'This is how I would mark them,' he continues as he pushes the sheet on the table towards me.

I pick up the sheet and take a look at it. The numbers vary only from zero to three. I look at the sheet carefully. He has marked them out of ten. Okay, I am confused! I thought my students were doing well.

'But I ... was happy ... they were turning in work. And I thought they were turning in *good* work,' I say.

'The work they are turning in is *shit*. It's worse than a badly painted movie poster,' he says. He does not sound happy.

I am not happy to hear what he is saying either. It's rather rude, insensitive, inappropriate and unfair to call the student's work shit. They might not have the best work, I agree, but they are trying for sure!

He looks at me as my expression changes from mildly curious to outraged and pops a piece of chocolate in his mouth and starts chewing on it.

'I will work harder with the students, sir. I have already been putting in a lot of time in with the students. Not only for the students of my own class, but also for students from other batches,' I say.

'Maybe that is the problem,' he says, chewing on his chocolate. 'Maybe you are indulging too much with the students. And maybe you are wasting too much time on other students when you should be working harder with your own.'

What the hell is his big fat problem!

~

It's evening. Pranav and I are in the market again having momos. It has become a daily ritual now. Every evening we go out to have momos.

'Sir-ji, do you have a girlfriend?' Pranav asks.

What has happened to him all of a sudden I don't know. And why does he need to ask me now, when the break-up is all too fresh. I can share that with him. Why should I lie or hide it? We all get into relationships and then break up. We are all human at the end of the day—we are all the same.

'I had one, we just broke up a few days back,' I say as if I don't feel any pain as I speak.

'Why, sir-ji, what happened?' he asks.

'We had our differences,' I say. 'We just grew apart.' I don't want to talk about it.

'Actually, sir-ji, I heard you fighting with someone on the phone. And you have been very upset after that.'

Is it? Am I that transparent? Damn it! I always thought I had a huge, strong wall around me to hide my emotions. Anyway, I don't want to discuss it. I want him to change the topic.

'I want to see her picture. Do you have her picture?'

I pull out my wallet and show him Nisha's photograph which I carry with me always. Yes, I am that pathetic a guy who carries his ex-girlfriend's picture in his wallet. But I swear I was going to take it out, tear it and flush it down the toilet tonight—seriously.

'She is beautiful, sir-ji!' he says looking at the picture. 'I hope you thought twice before breaking up with her,' he adds as I remember how painful the whole thing was.

Okay, enough is enough! I want to change the topic.

'Pranav, what do you want to do with your life?' I ask, looking at the momos on the plate with unseeing eyes.

'I want to earn money. I want to earn lots and lots of money,' he says through a mouthful of momos.

I look at him for a few seconds, my mind pushing me to say what I've been wanting to. 'Whatever you buy or own with the money that you earn, a BMW, an Audi, a Rolex, whatever ... there will always be the possibility that people will snatch it away from you. And you may never get it back. You should try to gain and earn things that no one can take away from you, that will stay with you for life and beyond,' I say as Pranav looks at me baffled.

After staring at me in silence for few seconds, he finally asks, 'For example?'

'For example, your memories, your experiences, your achievements and, most importantly, your work. These are the things no one can ever take away from you. These are the things that will stay with you forever. People will remember you for these things even after your death. And only these are your true earnings. Only these will bring you true happiness and deeper satisfaction that will stay with you for life.' As I say the words I remember the girl who taught me this—once upon a time.

~

I have a deal with the courier guy. If I am not home, he calls and asks me if he should leave the packet or take it back with him. He called today and I know there is a packet waiting for me. Pranav and I reach home around 5.30 p.m. I hastily open the door when Pranav asks me, 'Kya, sir-ji, very eager to go inside today. Anything special?'

'You'll see,' I smile.

I open the door and see an envelope lying on the floor. I pick it up.

It's from my publisher. I rip it open—it's my royalty cheque for the year. Hands trembling with excitement, I unfold the cheque and get the shock of my life. That's it? He has paid me

Rs 85,210 only! He has paid me Rs 85,210 for the whole year
for a book that has not only been appearing on bestseller lists
all over the country but also been among the top hundred titles
in Tellson's Book Count India right through! This is crazy!!
This is *insane*! He is cheating me nice and proper. Okay, that's
it! Enough is enough! I am going to open my own publishing
house. I am going to publish my own book; then no one will be
able to cheat me. And maybe this is the way of the future—self
publishing; just like independent film making. They get all the
awards these days. Remember *The Hurt Locker*? I am sure all
authors are soon going to open their own publishing houses
and just put an end to the miseries caused by these ... these ...
cheating, arrogant and snobbish publishers (all of whom must
burn in hell by the way).

'What happened, sir-ji?' Pranav has caught my expression.

'Nothing, I just got my royalty cheque,' I say.

'Show me, show me!' he jumps.

I pass it on to him. He gasps, 'Wow? Eighty-five grand! You
are a rich man, sir-ji!'

'Not a rich man, Pranav. This is my full year's earning.
People earn this much in a bloody month!'

I want to kill myself. I want to jump off the ledge of a really
tall building. This is shameful. I am almost twenty-seven, my
friends are thinking about becoming managers and CEOs and
... God! I don't even want to acknowledge this is real.

'Sir-ji, tell me one thing. I keep seeing all the other authors
in newspapers and magazines. Why don't you ever appear
there?'

'Because it's a dirty business, Pranav.'

'So tell me na, sir-ji.'

I collapse on the couch, sigh and say, 'Sit.' Pranav sits down. Maybe I shouldn't do it, maybe I should let him live with his illusions for a while. But for some reason I can't stop myself from telling him how the media and this industry works.

'The media is all sold,' I start. 'No newspaper or magazine will write anything about you unless you pay them. All the headlines about Kacchan's granddaughter's eye colour and his daughter-in-law's … mall appearance are bought. They have publicists and PR people working for them who take big money to get all this printed in the papers.'

He is looking at me with his eyes fixed, listening attentively. 'I was very naive when my first book was released. I believed the world was all about flowers and butterflies. I went to so many newspaper offices and met so many journalists. I presented my book to them and asked them to review it. They all noded very nicely and promised to surely write a review. But week after week went by and no reviews appeared. I started calling them and they either said yeah, they were going to finish reading the book and write the review soon or that they were running out of space and were not able to fit in the review. And when I picked up their papers, all they were writing about was which actor was dating whom and who was wearing a bikini and who was building six pack abs. I had a talk with my publisher then. He told me that if I want them to write about me, be it in the *Indian* or the *Hindustan Express* or the *Indian Times*, I would have to pay them. I detested the idea. If I paid them to write for me, they would never write what they genuinely felt about me, they would only write to please me. I felt they were behaving like writing whores. And I wanted to stay away from them. I didn't want to have anything to do with them thereafter. Even if a journalist approached me for an interview. I refused. I never said yes for any event or a book launch, unless it was not covered by the media.'

Pranav looks at me silently. He wants to say something and finally speaks up.

'But, sir-ji, without publicity how will your books sell? How will people get to know about them?'

'They've been selling as much as I want them to. I am not going to crush my ethics to increase the sale of my books,' I say. And that is true, my books have been selling. It's just that my publisher is not paying me for it.

31

**And she would not let him slide his hand under her
T-shirt—Karun**

And so it has come true. I am in a cinema hall with Lovanya
watching a movie. To attain anything in life you only need to
be persistent, all the rest follows. We are here to watch *The
Dark Knight Rises*, the movie that is set to smash all box-office
records. We are sitting in the corner seats, third row from the
back. There is still time for the show to start and people are
coming in, searching for their seats and settling down. Lovanya
is sipping the large Coke that we bought from the food counter
outside; she does not want to share. She is looking lovely and
I do not want to take my eyes off her.

'Karun, why do you want a girlfriend?' she asks. Something
in her voice tells me that she is aware of my staring at her and
my feelings. The answer to her question is simple. One needs
to not only satisfy emotional needs but also physical needs
after a certain age—that is the way of the world. It is so hard
right now to keep myself from touching her. But there is no

way I can tell her that. I know for a fact that a girl will never be with a guy if he reveals his true feelings. I hold her right hand with both my hands and squeeze it gently, 'Because I want a companion for life. Because I want to grow old with someone I always want to see happy.'

She looks at me and smiles. Her eyes tell me that she does not completely believe me. 'I read your book,' she says, 'I didn't know you waited outside my house under the gulmohar tree every evening to see me come into the balcony and talk to Deepti.'

The lights have dimmed and they are screening the trailer of *Ice Age: Continental Drift*.

'I have poured my heart out in my novel,' I say looking into her eyes. I know there has been all this talk about *boys being boys* and the idea of girls having their heart beneath their breasts and boys having their heart between their legs. But I don't really believe that. One, I think girls crave and think about sex as much as boys do. Two, even if it were true that boys are more driven by sex than girls, there is nothing wrong with it when the boy is committed to the girl and takes care of her, keeps her happy and fulfils all her demands, physical and emotional.

She holds my hand with her left hand and gives it a gentle shake, takes a deep breath and rests her head back on the blue velvet cushion of the seat.

This is good, she understands me. We are compatible.

They are screening some stupid 555 Golden Chai ad I am not at all interested in watching. I slowly put my arm around her shoulder and turn to look at her. She too turns and looks at me. There is a moment of silence and there is electricity in the air. I move my head a little forward and gently kiss her on her lips. She does not resist. Her lips are soft and firm and the watermelon gloss on her lips tastes sweet. I look at her firm round breasts under her grey top. I want to put a hand on them and feel them. If only we were not in a cinema hall but in some place more private. Something in my mind tells me that I should stop but it's impossible to hold back now. I merely brush my hand against her right breast when the lights go off and the theme music of the *Batman* movies starts playing. Lovanya puts a hand on my chest and pushes me back. 'Can we please watch the movie?' she says.

'Sure,' I shrug and rest my head back against my seat. Did I cross line? Did I offend her? Was this too early a move? I look at her from the corner of my eye and want to see the expression on her face. But it's too dark to figure out anything.

32

The red-hot and steamy sex incident in the hotel room in the mountains—Jeet

Her manuscript is around eighty per cent complete. It's the story of a fiery love affair between a journalist and a novelist wDé egos clash and wDé attraction for each other is manifested as a powerful tussle between them. It's only towards the end of the story that they both end up having somewhat violent sex and actually get together. Neeti is having a problem writing the 'power of sex' chapter. (That is what I think we should call it, but Neeti keeps insisting we call it 'The Power of Love Making'.)

My Shimla book event was four days ago but we have decided to stay on for another week, simply because it's wonderful to stay in the mountains. (Next stop: Chandigarh.) We go for a walk every evening to the ridge, which is a magnificent place. We've been to the old church where the end of the movie *Black* was shot and then to the Indian Institute of Advanced Studies, the building that was shown as the university in the same movie. There is something enchanting about that building sitting majestically on the top of the mountain. Amongst the first buildings in the north to get electrified this one still has an electrifying effect on many. Tall broad mountains surround it and it's so peaceful and soothing just to be there. Although I can't write poetry, being in such a place, I can imagine how the beauty of nature must have inspired countless poets through the ages. The tall deodar trees with their branches spreading like open palms catch the bright sunlight which leaves a golden glow on them. The mountains beyond the valley seem so close, yet so far. And such clear blue skies, they're an impossibility in the plains.

After our walk, we go back to the hotel every day and discuss the story we are working on. We are in my room right now and, if you look around, it looks like a book dumping yard. There are piles of books on the floor, on the chair, on the table, on the bed—everywhere. I can say without any exaggeration that we have bought all the Mills and Boon titles available at the Red Book Store in Shimla, where we had my book event, and have been reading the books recklessly since then—day and night. We take only one break a day and that is the evening walk together. We even order our food in the room, no breaks for lunch or dinner. After going through some seventeen books, we can say there is nothing that we have really found impressive. Right now, I am reading this weird book in which a guy has kidnapped a girl only because he found her pretty and cute. He ill treats her by tearing off her clothes and humiliating her but does not actually have sex with her till *she* wants to and says yes. From what I understand, the book says that the girl liked being dominated but takes time to accept it. It's like the darker parts of the mind are being explored here.

Anyway, on a serious note, it's actually quite difficult to read these books with a girl by your side. While reading them, you keep feeling horny and have to constantly shift and turn as you don't want her to know what's going on in your underpants. All the characters in these books keep having sex so freely that I am beginning to think that a) we should have more freedom in life and casual sex should not be looked down upon and everyone should be free to have it, and b) these books are so unrealistic and things don't happen so easily in real life. Believe me, I know how hard I have to try to win it each time. There are no handsome playboys in this world who get it so easily with just the flash of a smile. It's only a myth. I am sure.

I have been reading for two hours straight. Frankly, I have not read so many books in my entire life as I have in the past three days. I don't dig reading much. But I can't let Neeti realize that. That would completely ruin my image in her eyes. I need a break from reading for a few minutes; I want to relax my eyes. I turn around and look at Neeti. She is deeply engrossed in a book that has a picture of a vampire with his fangs showing and a woman dressed as a bride. *Bride of the Blood Suckers* the title reads. I do not want to disturb her. Maybe we will find some inspiration in that book and get some ideas for the chapter we need to write.

I get up from the bed and walk over to the window. The vast landscape stretches out—mountain ranges lined one behind the other and towering, snow-covered 'monsters' glittering in the afternoon sun beneath the spread of the cool, blue sky. I fill my lungs with the fresh and fragrant mountain air and let it out slowly.

Reading these books is not going to help. If we were to get an idea from reading these books, we would have got it by now.

'This reading is not helping. It's not giving me any ideas,' I say as I turn around and look at Neeti.

She looks up from her book and keeps it aside. She does not say anything.

'Maybe we should try something different. Maybe we should watch movies instead of reading books,' I say pointing to all the books lying around us.

She keeps staring at me.

'Or maybe we should try to imagine a situation and try to enact a scene!' I say excited. That's a great idea for sure.

She keeps staring at me still and then finally asks, 'But what would be the set-up?'

'Okay, see … There is this writer and this journalist and they both have sparks flying all over the place but their egos only turn that into hot … umm … clashes between them.'

'Hmm.'

'So this writer dude is in his hotel room after his big book launch in … Shimla!' Why can't we take inspiration from reality? 'His book launch was at the Gaiety Theatre. The one that Raj Kapoor's family got restored.'

'Okay.'

'His hotel is next to the Mall Road, it's a big lavish one.'

'Right.'

'This journalist chick, since she has a thing for him, has followed him here and calls him up and asks for an interview.'

'Hmm.'

'She plans to defame him by publishing nasty things about him, that's her way of gaining his attention.'

'Okay.'

'But he has no idea about her intentions and calls her over to his room for the interview.'

'Okay.'

'And by the end of the interview, they end up having sex!'

'Okay.' She thinks for a while and then says, 'Now the question is what kind of sex would they have, active or passive?'

'Meaning?'

'Would it be hot sex or soft sex?'

What kind of sex would they like? Now that is the question.

After a while she speaks up, 'They are both hot-tempered people. They would definitely like hot sex.'

'Cool! Let's enact this. I am here,' I say as I pick up a pile of books from the couch and put them with the other books on the table. 'And you have just come into this room for the interview.'

'Okay.'

'Shoot.'

'Jeetander,' she shoots in a fiery tone, 'there's a huge buzz everywhere that you are a womanizer and go around with a new girl every month. Is there any truth in the rumour?'

I flash a cocky smile and say, 'Girls keep throwing themselves at me. What kind of man would I be to keep rejecting them?'

Neeti pretends to jot something down and then looks up at me again.

'Your last book was about a love affair between two young

girls. The critics said the book lacked depth at many levels and gave a very superficial, misleading and rather fake idea about lesbian relationships. What do you have to say in your defence?'

She is really good at offending people. I look around the room for a while and spot a can of beer lying on the table in front of me. I pick it and offer her, 'Beer?'

'No, thank you, Mr Jeetander.'

'Okay,' I stare at her. Her hair is all messed up and she is wearing this loose sleeveless T-shirt and a pair of dark grey sweatpants. She has fire in her eyes and is looking super sexy in a very raw way. I actually feel like ripping all her clothes off, like the guy in the book I just finished reading and have mad sex with her.

'Mr Jeetander, would you please answer my question?'

'Yes, sure,' I say as I deliberately shake the can and open it. The beer erupts in a fountain of fizz that I deliberately spill on my shirt.

'Oh, I am so sorry. Just a minute,' I say as I quickly take off my shirt, sit back on the couch again and flex my muscles. 'So, what were you asking?'

'I was saying, Mr Jeetander, that your descriptions of a lesbian relationship in your previous book faced severe criticism,' she says as she runs her eyes over my body and gulps. 'Your comments on that.'

'What can I say? They said what they wanted to, can't do anything about it,' I shrug.

'Many people call you a "man slut". How do you feel about that?'

I stare at her for a few seconds and then say, 'Has anyone ever called you a slut?'

'Mr Jeetander!' she thunders.

I look at her intensely. Her body is tempting and teasing me. I am getting a hard-on again. Her firm, round breasts and her slim waist, I want to take her in my arms and kiss her all over.

'I said, has anyone ever called you a slut?' I repeat.

Without a warning, she gets up from her chair and slaps me tightly on my face. I feel my cheek burning from the impact. I look at her as she stands in front of me breathing heavily. I get up, hold her head with my hands and give her a firm kiss on her lips. She kisses me back.

I slide my hand under her T-shirt and caress her back and her waist. She kisses me even more passionately, holding me tight. I pull her T-shirt off, push her on the bed and kiss her from her belly up to her neck. She unbuttons my jeans and puts her hand inside.

It's happening! It's finally happening!

33

To destroy some, some should collaborate—Karun

It's a lazy Saturday afternoon and I don't have school today. This is why I have picked this day to mark the beginning of the execution of my grand plan. I have decided who my partner in crime is going to be and we are gonna rock. Devika is coming over today. It's 3 p.m. and she will be here any minute. She said she was going to come after lunch.

My laptop and my PC are both ready and waiting for me to begin the game.

The doorbell rings precisely at 3.07 and I rush to open the door.

'Hello,' I say with a gracious smile.

'Hey,' Devika smiles back. She is wearing a tight red top and a maroon cotton skirt with a flair that ends about three inches above her knees. For how she looks like right now, hot is an understatement.

'Come in.' I say as I unlock the mesh screen door.

She steps in and takes a good look around. It's a normal

house that I live in. The three-bedroom flat has three balconies—one each with two of the rooms and one with the kitchen. My mom, who is out for work right now (same as my dad by the way), has a taste for antiques. So the drawing room has some artefacts that are older than even my great-great-grandfather maybe. If you ask me, these are only pieces of junk lying all around the house but my mom can't stop caring about them.

'Quite an antique collection you have,' Devika says.

'You like them?' I ask.

'Sorry, but I don't have a thing for old stuff or for old people. No offence.'

'None taken,' I say as I lead her to my room, 'And FYI, I am no fan of the old either.'

'We have things in common then,' she says as she flashes a smile.

'We sure do.'

We enter my room and she throws her bag on my bed.

'Make yourself comfortable,' I say as she goes and sits on the bed and looks at me.

I smile. She smiles back and looks around at all the posters I have on my wall. No one can deny it. I have a killer collection of posters—*Dexter* (the one with splashes of blood which look like the wings of an angel), *Game of Thrones* (the one with Lord Eddard sitting on the iron throne with Ice in his hands), *The Godfather* and so many more.

'Nice collection of posters, I must say,' she says, turning back at me.

'Thanks,' I smile.

'One thing is common in all these TV shows and movies, I must say—conspiracies and violence. They all are very dark,' she says.

'I know. And that is how the world is. Everyone is hungry for power. Friends stab you in the back, people conspire against you. The weak are eaten by the strong, that is the law of nature,' I say.

She looks back at me with her eyes fixed on me, 'Don't you think you get too carried away by all these shows and movies?'

It's only foolish to expect people to understand you. I look back at her silently for a few seconds and ask, 'Would you like to have something?'

'Just a Coke will do.'

'One Coke coming right away,' I say as I turn around and head for the kitchen.

'And don't even think about spiking my drink. You won't live to see the world the same way again if you do that,' I hear her say.

Her comment hits me a little. I had no such intentions, but I want to play a little with her now. I turn around and say, 'What if I do?'

'I have a little knife in my bag. I know how to use it on boys.'

'Are you threatening me?'

'No,' she replies plainly, 'I am warning you.'

'I like your courage.'

'I would suggest you never test it,' she says, looking at me in the eyes. I look back at her and there is silence for a while.

I like her. She is more interesting than I thought she would be.

'Let me get you what you asked for,' I say with my eyes fixed on her and walk out of the room.

I come back to my room with two cans of chilled Coke and I see my awards record book in her hands. It's a simple record of all the authors in India who have won the Bang Bang Award for Indian popular fiction in the past ten years—since the award was established. It's the biggest honour for the popular fiction writers in India. The book has detailed biographies of all the authors who have ever won this award along with the details of all their books—the ones that they won for and the ones that they did not win for.

Devika notices me entering the room and smiles, 'So this is your aim—the Bang Bang Award?'

'You're a sneaky girl, but pretty smart, I must say.'

'Do you really think you will be able to beat Chirag Barot for his award count ever? He has won this award four times already.'

'I will beat him, and everyone else like him. You wait and see,' I say.

We are drinking chilled Coke now and are well over our previous conversation. But somehow we are still sitting in silence. We must not waste time. We must discuss what we met today for.

'My plan is,' I say, breaking the ice, 'to attack our enemy's psychology.'

She is looking at me. She is paying attention.

'What we are gonna do is create fake email ids and send hate mail to all the authors who are being published by Dash right now. Hate mails so strong that they will want to kill themselves after reading them.'

I have sent a few such mails already, including a really strong one to Rohit. I bet it must have shaken him up—he is such a softie.

Devika is looking and me and does not even blink.

'And that is not all. We are also going to post really rotten reviews for their books on all the online bookstores,' I add.

'Oh Karun, this is despicable!' she says looking at me and falls silent.

What does she mean? Is she not up with my idea?

Suddenly she begins to laugh and says, 'And I love it!'

34

**As he is sitting at home in his pajamas, struggling
to develop the plot for his next story, he has no idea
about the ideas others are plotting—Rohit**

I am home and beating my brain for a plot for my next book.
People have this whole glamorous idea about authors and
they are terribly wrong. Authors are mostly just sitting in their
homes, shabby, unshaven, with overgrown hair, constantly
cursing themselves for being so dumb and and incapable of
getting a story right. Scratching my head, I look away from my
computer screen and see Pranav sitting in a corner, staring at
me with a notebook on his lap. He is supposed to be working
on his assignment but is only staring at me and not writing
anything.

'Sir-ji, can I ask you something.'

'Okay,' I say.

'You always keep working? You never rest?' he asks, tilting
his head to one side.

That is not true. I do not work all the time. I waste a lot of time, I waste my time like crazy. But I do believe in the simple mantra of 'work is worship'. Firmly. And that is because when I was in the second standard I had made a chart on it for the classroom notice board. It was while writing those words that the maxim turned into belief, one that grew stronger each time I looked at the chart in my classroom. But I don't give him the long explanation.

'Well, I believe that work is worship, so …' I say looking at him. Maybe, my saying this to him will teach him to believe too. 'And people who don't think so, I find them quite irritating.'

Actually, I am only being polite, I don't find such people irritating—I simply hate them.

'You must find me very irritating then,' Pranav says.

'I used to,' I look at him and smile.

As I look back at my laptop screen, the silence in the room is shattered by the screaming ringtone of my cell phone.

I pick up the phone and the screen flashes 'Karun Mukharjee'. We exchanged numbers a few days back and he has been calling quite frequently since then. He keeps asking me for tips on how to handle Mr D.K. Dé. We haven't discussed much about his writing though.

'Hello,' I take the call.

'Hello, bhaiya, how are you?'

'I am good, how are you?'

'I am good, bhaiya. Tell me one thing, what percentage royalty do you get?'

Is this something I should share with him? 'Why, what happened?' I ask.

'I don't know, bhaiya. I have been talking to Mr Dé regularly about my book and you know the kind of things he keeps talking about and how hard it is to shake him off,' he says.

'Ha ha! I know.'

'Yesterday he finally gave me an offer and I signed the contract, five per cent royalty.'

'That's it? Only five per cent? This guy is a total thief!' Just then I hear a beep on my phone.

'Hey, just wait a minute,' I say, 'I think I am getting a call.'

I check the screen but there is no call waiting. I wonder what that beep was.

'Yeah,' I say, 'it was nothing. So you were saying?'

'No, you were saying … ?' he says, 'That he is a thief …'

'Oh yes, he is a thief. Not only is he going to cheat you with the number of copies sold, he is only going to pay you for one-third the quantity he sells and give you only five per cent royalty. This man should burn in hell I tell you!' There is a beep again on the phone but no call waiting when I check.

Given what Karun has just told me, I am infuriated.

'You know, he is such a crook. I had a word with him over the phone just a few days back. That parasite! I was so angry at him! He put my second book in the market without informing me. That asshole! Thankfully I somehow convinced him to increase the print run for my first book. God only knows how I put sense into that pot-head to make him understand that simple logic.'

'Yeah, okay, bhaiya, I got to go now. I will catch you later.'

'Okay, bye. And best of luck for your new book.'

'Thank you, bhaiya, you are the best!'

35

And he has acquired his weapon for someone's destruction—Karun

YES! This is the day!! This is the day I have been waiting for for the longest time. I have recorded Rohit saying terrible things about Mr Dé in his own voice. All I need to do now is send the conversation I recorded to Mr Dé and Rohit will be history. Mr Dé will kick Rohit out of the publishing house himself. This is simply wicked! Bye-bye, Mr Rohit Sehdev, once hotshot author, it's time to kiss goodbye to your writing career.

36

The sexy beasts are sexier and hornier than ever before—Jeet

Life is just full of kicking action these days. After Neeti and I had sex that day, it's like the floodgates have opened. Each time we look at each other we feel like making out again. Each time I look at her, I feel like holding her and kissing her till I am out of breath. And she looks extra beautiful these days. I don't know if it's just me or if she has actually started dressing differently. The other day, she wore that little black dress and the mere sight of her gave me a tingle between my legs and activated my merchandise. Life is so beautiful and fulfilling when you are physically intimate with someone. It just makes everything seem ... whole again. It makes you feel that everything is complete. Neeti has finally decided to take up one room instead of two.

'We don't need two rooms,' she said yesterday. 'Most of the time we are working on our book in your room. We are just paying extra money to the hotel.'

And why would I have any problem with that? I agreed instantly. I just warned her about one thing, 'It's totally okay with me but I am used to being only in boxers in my room. I hope that's not a problem with you.'

She didn't have any problem with that. 'That's okay, there is nothing I have not seen before. Nothing that would surprise me,' she said.

Obviously, why would she have a problem with that? Why would she have a problem with looking at a well-toned, chiselled body?

We are still in Shimla. Neeti liked the place so much she said it would be a shame if we didn't spend at least ten days here.

We are some twenty minutes away from our hotel and are sitting by this small little stream that runs through the mountains here. The evening sun is imparting a golden hue. The shadows on the mountains are rising and the green foliage is tinged with the last golden glow of the day. The steady flow of the stream makes a soothing, gushing sound that seems to promise something at the same time. There is no one to disturb us and whole set-up is magical.

I am thinking how great it would be to just sit here and stare at the mountains, the trees and the blue sky with cottony white clouds. It's funny how Neeti met me a few weeks ago as a stranger and how we have been together since. A random trip during which she just wanted to let go before her wedding has resulted in a professional collaboration of sorts.

I turn to look at her and ask, 'When is your wedding planned, by the way?'

She looks at me and smiles, 'Early next year. Six months
away.'

'Cool. How did you meet him?'

'I didn't, my dad did. And then he *made* me meet him.' She
smiles, 'He is the sone of a friend of a friend. MBA from MDI,
Gurgaon. Runs his big, hotshot IT business with a turnover
of ten crore annually.'

'Okay.'

Silence.

'Do you like him? I mean …you are marrying him, do you
love him?' I ask hesitantly.

She lets out a little laugh and says, 'No arranged marriage
is based on love. They are all based on the guy's salary package
and the girl's abilities to cook food, clean the house and manage
guests and the guy's parents. No one cares if the guy turns out
to be an alcoholic or a mad man with uncontrollable anger
issues.' She looks down at the ground as she plucks blades of
grass and throws them away.

'And … you are okay with this?'

She looks at me and says, 'No.'

'Then you should do something about it.'

She smiles and says, 'It's too late now. If I refuse, my dad
will marry me off forcefully. I have only three options. Leave
the house now and stay independently. Run away during my
wedding and then start living independently somewhere. Or
marry this rich man and force myself to love him. The second
option involves good drama. That would be fun actually—
running away on your wedding day, just like in the movies.'

Suddenly, my phone starts to ring. I pull it out of my pocket and look at the screen. It's an unknown number. Who could this be? I wonder. I don't like it when random, unknown people call me for reasons that are only just stupid.

'Hello?'

'Hello, is this Jeet Obiroi?' a boy's voice asks.

'Yes, who is this?'

'Bhaiya, this is Karun. Remember, I emailed you and you gave me your number … '

It's that crazy kid from the Delhi book event.

'Hi, how are you?'

'I am good, bhaiya, how are you?'

'I am good.'

'Bhaiya, today is the happiest day of my life and I wanted to share my happiness with you, as you are someone I have always considered my guru.'

I smile, 'What's the big occasion?'

'The cover design for my book just got finalized today. It is so thrilling to see my dream becoming reality.'

'That is great, congratulations!'

'Thank you so much, bhaiya. You have no idea how much your wishes mean to me.'

'Okay,' I say as I give out a little laugh.

'Bhaiya, I need a little favour from you.'

'Tell me.'

'My book is in the editing process. It would mean a lot to me if you would go through my manuscript and give me your valuable comments and suggestions.'

Hmm … going through a whole manuscript is going to

take time. And Neeti and I need to finish the manuscript we are working on. I don't think I can afford to help him right now. Moreover, I don't even need him as co-author anymore. I have got one—a hot, sexy one. 'I am really sorry but I am really tied up these days,' I say.

I look at Neeti as her phone starts to ring. She takes it out of her pocket, gets up and walks away to take the call.

'It's okay, bhaiya, never mind. But you have to help me with my next book,' Karun says.

'Sure,' I smile.

'I had a long meeting with Mr Dé today. He is kind of weird.'

'Why, what happened?'

I can't deny that Dé is actually quite weird. When I contacted him for my manuscript, the first thing he asked me for was my picture.

'I don't know, he sounded as if ... as if he ... didn't like you much. He said that you are the most difficult author to handle and your books sell only because of the PR people you have hired and ...' he trails into silence.

'And what?'

That son of a bitch! I am going to thrust an elephant's dick in his fucking ass!

'I don't know how to say this ... but he said that your book is the worst book he has ever published.'

Fucking bastard!

'I am really sorry to tell you all this but I felt really angry when he was talking about you like this and I thought you should know.'

'That's okay. You don't have to be sorry about it. He is an asshole, I know. But I'm glad you told me.'

'No problem, bhaiya, I have to go now. It's time for my math tuition. Will call you later sometime?'

'Sure, bye.'

'Bye, bhaiya.'

I hang up and find it hard to control the anger flaring inside me. That fucking asshole, how could he talk about me like that?

37

The exchange of the horrible emails—Rohit

Dear Rohit,

This is in continuation to our telephonic conversation the other day.

More or less I found myself insulted by your words and thus am writing you this mail. We do not want to bind any authors with us and request you to look for some better publisher who can give you more facilities and distribution network.

We are a very small publisher and happy with our own way of publishing and do not want any third person's suggestions regarding our modules of operation.

We wish you best of luck.

D.K. Dé

What the hell does he mean? *He* felt insulted? This is

outrageous! What kind of a publisher is he if he finds my request to promote my books an insult? He cheats me out of money that he owes me, refuses to show me the accounts for the sales of my books, releases my book without informing me, gives me false, lame and dishonest answers to anything I ask him and he says he felt insulted by what *I* said? This is insane! This is totally insane! I don't want to work with him. Good, that he has asked me to find a better publisher for myself.

I hit the reply tab.

Dear Sir,

   I was quite shocked to read your mail.

   Frankly speaking, I do not recall saying anything offensive to you during our conversation on the phone the other day.

   On the other hand, after the conversation, I felt quite happy, satisfied and relieved to know that things were well on track and we had had a rather fruitful discussion about my books.

   I have always had full faith in you and great respect for you. But despite repeated requests for the clarification of the account statements, I have received no information from your end. I still firmly believe that I deserve an answer.

   As an author, it is very unsettling for me to know that my publisher is upset with me during the release of my second book and

is stating that he is a small publisher,
has fixed modules of working and addresses
the author as a 'third person' for his own
intellectual property.

I request you to stop publishing both my
books and clear the outstanding amounts.

Warm regards,

Rohit Sehdev

Bloody asshole!

38

**If he thinks no one can fool him, he is only being
foolish—Karun**

We wrote a total of thirty-five hate mails and forty-three bad
reviews for five books. This is what one of the hate mail reads
like,

```
I donno whether u hv time 2 luk at ur reader's
mails o not,bt,,your DOS THINGS 'IN LYF BG
N SML',,!!,,dt buk draggd me here 2 write
u smthng,,,many people must hv appreciated
ur wrk as i hv seen 'NATIONAL BESTSELLER'
on top of dat,,,bt seriously dear,,dat
'SUCKS',,m so sry m sayng dis,bt dat buk
hs nthng 2 read bout.,,i totly wasted ma
100bucks on dat,!!dis ws d worst buk i hv
evr cum across....!!
so plzzzzzz,,,,i beg,,,DON EVR WRITE ANY
NOVEL,,U HAVE NO SENSE OF IT,,I BET I CN
```

```
WRITE A FAAAAR BETTER STORY THN OF URS...!!
hope u'l tk my words seriously,,as
m actly dead serious n so frustratd
after ending ur so cald 'novel',,,!
sry if hv been d 1s critic 4 ur nationl
bestseller:p...bt m sure many ppl out here
feels d
same,,,ehheh!!
gud luck!!!
nt expctng ur reply,,n wud b shockd if u
do so,,!!
take care buddy,,,bbye
```

And this is what one of the reviews read like.

I HATED THIS BOOK TO THE CORE. @AUTHOR
PLEASE SPARE US THE HORROR OF GOING
THROUGH ANOTHER ONE OF YOUR BOOKS. GIVE
UP WRITING.
I would recommend everybody to refrain from buying this
book. Please don't. It is a story told in the most boring way,
makes no sense and to top it all does not have a story at all.

And another one reads like this:

I bought the book on a whim, as I kind of liked the synopsis
on its cover. But this book was such a drag. The total lack
of proper sentence structure, bogus writing and a really
stupid plot is what the book is all about. It's such a shame

that those who don't have even an iota of writing skill are getting published. People buy these books just because it costs less than Rs 100. Better save that money for the likes of Chirag Barot. This author is a total Wannabe. One can ignore slight grammatical errors, but a book filled with nonsense written in the worst way, is too hard to digest even more the most patient readers. I never leave a book in the middle, nor skip pages. But this book tested the limits of my patience. I had to finish the book as I wanted to be fair to the hard-earned money that I spent on this book. I literally feel like throwing this book in the garbage. STAY AS FAR AWAY FROM THIS BOOK AS POSSIBLE. Or better yet. Go to a bookstore and read just the first two pages, and if you still buy it, then may God help you.

I read the review again and a smile creeps up on my face. The things that we have written are so wicked that it would shake the life out of any author. And it wouldn't have been half as good if Devika hadn't been with me. She is a killer, man!

It's lunch time at school and we, Devika and I, are sitting outside the school canteen. We are going to release these mails and reviews slowly—one or two every three days. The first batch goes out today and we are sitting with our laptops to do precisely that. The funniest thing is that the fake profiles and fake email addresses we created were using the names of the characters from the authors' own novels. Just that one author's character is going to say bad things to another author. It's quite artistic and poetical in its own way, like igniting a war between the imaginary and the real.

'The wi-fi is torturously slow today,' Devika says.

'Yes, it is,' I say without looking away from my laptop screen. I avoid looking at her. Just the sight (or even the thought of her, at times) gets me all sexed up.

After a minute's silence, she speaks up again, 'How's it going between you and Lovanya?'

'Great. Thank you for asking,' I reply.

She turns towards me, puts the screen of her laptop down, smiles and says, 'Liar.'

'Excuse me?'

'Neither of you is meant for the other. You are someone who would sell his soul to the devil for glamour and success and she is someone who worships G-O-D. She might pretend to be all that but I know what she is like deep down inside. And even *you,* for that matter, know that. You are evil incarnate but she is a good person.'

'That is not true,' I say looking her in the eye.

'Keep telling yourself that.'

Silence.

'And I have seen how you look at me. Your strong physical desires are so evident. And there is no way Lovanya is ever going to let you even touch her. There is no way your relationship will survive.'

'Shut up.'

She just smiles and looks at me.

'In fact, even right now you are not as interested in her as you used to be … Or for that matter as interested as you are in me,' she says as she arches her back elegantly and thrusts her bust out. 'For the past so many years, your biggest agenda for the day was to have lunch with her. And today you are sitting here with me outside the school canteen.'

'That is because we have got work to do together.' I say.

'Yeah right, Karun. But do think of another excuse when I ask you the same question later,' she says as she smiles.

I stare back at her and can't think of anything to say as she stares back at me. She is taking over my mind. And she knows it.

'Now get me a packet of chips. I am hungry,' she says.

~

Karun goes to the canteen to get a packet of chips. Devika waits till he is out of sight and picks up his laptop. His personal Gmail account still logged in—perfect. Immediately, she types a mail to her own Gmail account from his account:

```
Dear Devika,

    It's been happening to me since the day
we met at the cycle stand after school. I
can't get you out of my mind. I think about
you day and night. I think I like you. No,
wait; what I feel for you is stronger than
that. I think I am in love with you. I used
to think I was in love with Lovanya but now
I know it was nothing close to love. It was
just a ... teenage infatuation, a fling, a game
that my mind was playing with me just to
have fun. We have so much in common—we  have
```

```
the same career aims, same interests. We are
compatible at all levels. We are meant for
each other.
   I am writing this to you because I wanted
you to know how I feel about you. And I want
to know how you feel about me.
   Yours,
   Karun
```

After she has finished typing, she reads the mail again, smiles and clicks the send button. Then she goes to the 'sent items' folder and deletes the mail. It is a foolproof plan. No one will ever know that she sent the mail from Karun's account. She quickly puts the laptop exactly where Karun had left it.

She draws up her knees and rests her chin on them and watches the children playing in the school ground. There is innocence in their actions—running after their friends, chasing them, cracking jokes, laughing. There is innocence in all of us, she thinks. There is innocence even in Karun, no matter how smart and shrewd he might consider himself. It is his innocence that had made him trust Devika and he will never get to know what she has just done.

39

When an author gets an email with slapping threats—Rohit

It's going good, it's all going fine. I take criticism positively. I did not take Jabba the Hutt's words personally (I totally hate him by the way. No wait, not hate; loathe, I loathe him). I am working harder with my students now and his fat self will see the result very soon. Pranav has not been working much lately though. He has been in *relax* mode for all of last week, watching TV, having momos, sleeping or spending time on Facebook. But it's okay, I think—everyone needs a break once in a while.

I push open the door of the faculty room and march towards my cabin when I hear the HOD call my name, 'Rohit, can I have a word with you for a minute?'

'Sure, ma'am.'

I go to her cabin and she asks me to sit, shifting her laptop to the side and looks at me.

'How's Pranav doing?' she asks straight.

'Okay. He is doing okay,' I say.

'Each year, the dean expels a few students from college due to their performance. He prepares a hit-list as he calls it,' she says.

'Oh.'

'He went to your class,' she continues, 'and he was particularly unhappy with Pranav's performance.' She is looking at me with keen eyes. 'It's an internal, secret matter but since you have been working with him, I thought I would let you know.'

'Thank you.' This means danger. This is not good news.

'I wanted to make sure that he is working fine. Working enough not to be expelled.'

'Oh yes, he is totally working,' I lie, 'there is nothing whatsoever to worry about.'

I must make him work! I must make him work now. It's red-alert time!

~

I walk out of the faculty hall dazed. I need some fresh air. I took the full responsibility for one kid and that very kid is on the hit-list. This is terrible! He is going to fail and he is going to be thrown out of college and spend a degree-less and jobless life and it's all going be my fault. I am going to be the one responsible for ruining his life! But I shouldn't panic, I must stay calm and find ways to make him work again. I am walking in the corridor thinking about all this when I see a student sitting on the parapet with a book in her hands and the dean standing next to her. He spots me coming and calls, 'Rohit, come here.'

I march towards him.

'I didn't know you write,' Jabba says chewing the chocolate in his mouth; it has spread on his beard too.

I don't like it when people ask me this. They always start treating me differently after that and it's seldom for the better.

'Yes, sir,' I say, wishing I could just shrink or slip away as he stares at me with sharp eyes. 'I read a few pages, and I was telling her …,' he speaks with the chocolate in his mouth, spraying out a little as I look at him with anticipation. Did he like it? Does he think it is nice?

' … that it looks like a book best read in the toilet—you can shit it out as you read it. Ha ha ha!' He starts laughing and his belly shakes like a bowl full of jelly.

I want to punch him. I want to punch him in the face and give him a black eye and break his nose! If he doesn't like my writing, he can tell me what it lacks and how I can improve it. He is a bloody PhD for crying out loud—he must have written so much! He has no right to insult me in front of my students like that by saying he wants to flush it down the toilet. I want to flush *him* down the toilet.

He takes a step back and, before walking away, looks at me again and says, 'I didn't know you write.' This time he sprays some of the half-eaten chocolate on my face.

I stand there, shell-shocked. Is my writing that bad? Is it as bad as shit?

'Sir,' I hear a voice say.

I turn around and see it's the student who was sitting on the parapet.

'Don't mind what Dean Sir just said. I am reading your book and it's really funny.'

I nod and force a smile. Does she understand how terrible it feels when someone trashes your work like that?

~

I have hit rock bottom. I lie at the bottom of the ocean with no ray of hope touching me at all. There is no light at the end of the gloomy tunnel. In fact, all there is is a gloomy tunnel. There is a giant, solid, ice-covered wall front of me, like the one in *Game of Thrones* beyond which all the monsters lived, beyond which there is hell. My days used to be sunny and happy once. I used to be a star, people used to love me and my work. Now everyone hates me. They send me hate mail and slapping threats. I stare at the new hate mail I just received on my computer:

```
You are the biggest asshole I have ever come
across. You have no right to write such a
terrible book and get it published and make
people waste their money. Your book is the
worst book that has ever existed in the
history of mankind. It was so frustrating
to read this pathetic book of your that
when I was half way through it I wanted to
find you and hold you by your ear, slap you
repeatedly, yes, you read it right, slap
```

```
you repeatedly till your cheeks are red as
a monkey's ass, pull out your wallet from
your pocket and take my 100 rupees back that
I had wasted on your book.
    Stop writing! PLEASE STOP WRITING YOU
ASS-HOLE!
    Infinitely frustrated, irritated and angry,
    Ravish Kakkar


(Yes, I am telling you my name. I am not
scared to do so.)
```

I want to do something bad today. I want to do something that is bad for my health. I want to drink a Coke. I don't care if it dissolves my bones and makes a paunch pop out.

Maybe this reader is right. Maybe I should stop writing. Maybe my writing *is* terrible.

'What are you doing, sir-ji?' It's Pranav walking into the room.

'Nothing, it's just another hate mail. I get these all the time,' I sigh.

'Show me, show me,' he jumps.

I don't know what his big problem is? What is there to be so excited about? My life is coming to an end. I am overwhelmed by thoughts of suicide … I think I should stop living. How would people who send me these hate mails like it if I am found hanging from the fan with my tongue sticking out?

'Wow! Someone must really hate you to write this,' Pranav says after reading the mail.

'I am sure.'

'I want to read your book, sir-ji,' he says, looking at me.

Great, now even he is going to start hating me.

~

Pranav didn't go to college today. I gave him a huge scolding in the morning. He is so non-serious about everything, it's just not done! I actually locked him inside the house and took the key with me. He really needs to work on his painting. It's way more important than to attend one day in college. They are going to kick him out of college if he does not turn in a good submission for the final. But it's okay, he is a good kid, and an intelligent one. He is totally capable of creating a good painting. I turn the key and open the door. I am furious at what I see. Pranav is lying on the couch and watching a cricket match on TV. I say nothing and simply switch the TV off and stand in front of it, staring angrily at him.

'Sir-ji, IPL, final match, last over! *Please!*'

I must keep quiet, I must not say anything. I know if I start speaking I am going to be brutal. 'Pranav, get up and go work.' I order.

'Sir-ji, last, *please*, last over!'

'Pranav, do you realize how critical this time is for you? Do you understand how much is at stake right now? You are the most non-serious and irresponsible kid I have ever come across in my *whole life*.'

Pranav stands in front of me with a long face.

'You have been behaving really unreasonably and impossibly

lately, Pranav,' I thunder. 'You go missing for hours every day in the evening. You always come back with the same stories. I have been so patient with you.' Seriously ... that is quite a matter of worry for me. I don't know what he really is up to these days.

'I want you to go to your room and work,' I say with fire in my eyes. 'For at least four hours straight. I don't care even if you *die* of starvation. And if you come out any time before four hours, I WILL CHOP OFF YOUR FEET and feed them to the pigs!'

He just sits in front of me, listening to what I say but does not budge. I pause, try to maintain my calm and say, 'Understand that I mean business, Pranav. There is no way out today.' I stare at him angrily. Silent and meek, he gets up and walks to his room.

~

It has been a really bad day. Nothing is going right. I have spent the last three hours beating my brain to figure out a plot for my next novel; none of it makes sense or sounds sane. Writing a crime thriller or a murder mystery is the toughest job in the world. I need to take a break, seriously. I need to go on a vacation. Maybe I should stick to my genre and write a comedy. Yes, I should do that, I should write a comedy. And I should start my research now. I should read Nick Hornby! But what would be the plot? What would be the story? Damn it!

'Sir-ji.' I turn around to see Pranav peeping out of his room with only his head visible in the doorway. I look at the wall clock; it's only been three hours, 'Not before four hours at any cost, Pranav,' I say like a robot without even looking at him.

'Sir-*ji*,' he pleads.

I turn around, look at him and say, 'Pranav, do you realize …' But before I say anything more, he comes running,and hugs me tightly and says, 'Sir-ji, please! No scolding, please, sir-ji! I am hungry, sir-ji and I just can't work when I am hungry. Please let's go out and eat. I'll come back and work. I'll work the whole night. I promise, I promise.'

By god! I really don't know how to handle the kid!

~

I am about the open the gate when Pranav yells, 'Wait, sir-ji,' and comes running, jumping the gate in one smooth move.

'Your turn,' he says as he lands on the other side of the gate.

No way! There is no way on earth I am going to do what he is asking me to. I simply walk up to open the gate when he holds my hand and stops me.

'No, sir-ji, you have to jump today.' He insists as I stare back at him and say, 'Have you gone crazy? What is wrong with you?'

'Why are you always so strict about everything in life, sir-ji? We should do this … we should *not* do that. Why don't you ever let yourself free? Why are you always so uptight about everything?'

'I am not uptight!' He is stupid.

'Yes, you are.'

'No, I am not.'

'Prove it.'

'I don't need to,' I say as I free my hand to open the gate.

'Okay, I get it.'

'What?'

What's his problem? Why won't he back off?

'You don't want to jump because you can't—you are too old to do it.'

'No, I am not.' He knows nothing. I'll show him, I am *not* old! I think for a moment, make up my mind and say, 'Okay, show me once again how you jump.'

In one smooth motion he jumps and lands inside while I observe him closely. I take a few steps back to gain momentum.

'Wait,' he says suddenly. 'Let me go out,' he says as he jumps out. 'Now,' he signals.

'Okay, this is your plan to make me fall so that …'

'Sir-ji, we've been over this! Trust me, for once just trust me,' he interrupts me.

It's a four and a half feet jump. It's not impossible. I take a deep breath and run to the gate. I hold the top rail of the gate firmly with both my hands, lift myself up simultaneously and swing with my legs over the gate in one smooth motion. Just as I land on the other side of the gate, my foot slips and Pranav catches me.

'See, I can jump. I am *not* old,' I say, panting a little and regaining my balance.

'I know,' he smiles as he lets me go. 'And my plan was to make you jump, not to make you hurt yourself. It's not always true; not everyone's going to cheat you. There are always some people you can trust.'

~

At times a simple, meaningless act helps us cross major barriers in life. I only jumped over a gate yet I am feeling unbelievably free. We are walking to the momos stall when suddenly I hear a sharp, piercing whistle.

'By god, Pranav.' I don't know what's gotten into him. He has put two fingers in his mouth and is whistling in the middle of the road.

'Sir-ji, do you know how to whistle?'

'No.' Nisha always wanted me to whistle.

'It's very easy,' he says, 'just put the index finger of both your hands in your mouth and blow full.' He demonstrates with another sharp whistle.

I put both my index fingers in my mouth, do exactly what he did but only an awkward whoosh comes out.

I pull my fingers out and wipe off the saliva with a handkerchief.

'Keep practicing,' he laughs, 'it will happen.'

40

**When two worlds drift apart (which were
never one)—Karun**

It's been a while since I have spent time with Lovanya. So today
we are meeting in Pizza Hut. I am sitting here waiting for her
and she is expected any minute. I look at my watch; it's 1.20
p.m. We were supposed to meet at 1. After a few minutes, I
get bored and pull out my phone, plug in the earphones and
start watching the latest episode of *Dexter*. After another fifteen
minutes or so, I feel someone staring at me and look up to see
Lovanya standing in front of me.

'Hey!' I cheer up and stand.

'Hi,' she smiles.

We both sit and an awkward silence takes over. Neither of
us speaks and we hear only the music and the chatter of the
people around along with the sharp clutter of the cutlery.

'So, tell me, what's up these days?' I ask. It's actually been
three days since we talked to each other. I have been so busy
with my book and my plan.

'Nothing much. You tell me ...' she says, going through the menu.

'It's been crazy for me lately,' I sigh. Actually, I haven't even told her about the plan yet. And I am sure she is going to love it when I tell her. It's a genius plan and there is no denying it. *It's foolproof!* There is no better way to reach the top.

'Yeah, I can imagine. I've heard a lot of things about you lately.'

'Is it? Am I becoming popular or what!' I laugh.

'There is a difference between becoming popular and becoming notorious. If only you would understand that.'

'What you mean?' I stare at her.

'Nothing,' she simply shrugs.

This is not done. She has to tell me what she means by that. I won't let her dodge my question. I stare back at her demanding an explanation.

She looks at me in the eye and then turns back to the menu in front of her. After a while, without looking at me, she says, 'Don't tell me you don't know the things people are saying about you.'

'Like what?'

'Like how you and Devika are more than friends.'

'That is not true, I swear!'

'Really? And what about the kiss that happened between you and Devika behind the canteen yesterday?'

'What the hell are you talking about? Nothing like that happened!' What is she talking about? I have never kissed Devika! 'It's a false rumour, believe me.'

Lovanya rolls her eyes and says, 'Is it? That must also be a *false rumour* that Devika comes to your house every evening these days.'

'Yes, I mean no, that is true but she only comes because we are working together.'

'Really? What work, Karun?'

'Okay, I've wanted to tell you about this for a while now. It's pure genius.' Lovanya's eyes are fixed on me.

'When my book comes out in the market,' I continue, 'I want to make sure that I don't have any other author to compete with at Dash Publishers. So this is what I've done: I've created fake ids and posted as many bad reviews about their books as I could and sent them several hate mails.'

There is silence for a while and then she says, 'That is despicable, Karun.' She looks at me and continues, 'And I can't believe that you could think of something that disgusting!'

There is a moment's silence and then, almost as a reflex, I say, 'You are just jealous of my success, that's what you are.'

'Jealous? Me?' she lets out a little laugh. 'I can't believe this is coming from the guy who said that he wrote the whole book just for me and I was the reason for everything that was happening to him.'

'Things change, people change. Just like you.'

'I have changed?' She laughs, '*I have changed?* It's you who have changed, Karun, not me.'

'I was always like this. I am the same, just as I was.'

'Yes, maybe you are right. Only I was a little too blind to see that.'

'That's not *my* fault.'

'This is seriously insane. Why won't you just admit that you now like Devika who will let you do anything to her; not me, who will draw a line and keep you at a distance.'

'That is not true and you know that.'

'Oh come on! I have seen you two together. I have seen how you look at her.'

There is no point arguing, her belief is firm. I can't change the way she thinks now. But I want to hurt her. I want to hurt her for what she just said.

'Why don't you just accept that I have become *somebody* from a nobody in a matter of days? I have become more famous than you and you can't handle it.'

A smile that looks cruel to me curls on her face, 'You say you are famous. But do you realize that your fame has taken away all your friends? When was the last time you spoke to Ishan or Gaurav or even me for that matter? Do you even know what's going on in our lives? You have been busy working for your book you say. I hope you realize the price you are paying for your "work" and your "fame". What comes easily, goes away easily. That's a simple truth of life,' she says as I look back at her. 'But don't worry, you will learn it one day, maybe the hard way, but learn it you will.'

Hah! Cook all the stories you want. Throw all the gyan you like. I know that none of it is true, none of it makes sense. I don't even want to look at her. I turn my head and look outside the window.

'I read the mail, Karun, Devika showed it to me herself after I had denied what she was saying more than ten times.'

'What mail?'

'The mail that you wrote to her.'

'I never wrote her any mail.'

'Stop lying. I read it with my own eyes, Karun.'

'I am not lying, you are,' I snap. 'If you don't want to be with me anymore, why don't you just come out clean and say so? Making stories about mails.' I shake my head, 'So petty.'

'I was a fool, Karun, I was a fool to trust you,' she says looking at the table. 'And all the people who you think are your own right now, they are going to leave you.' She continues, 'And out of those, Devika is will be the first one. She is going to leave you as soon as she gets what she wants out of you. And then you will be alone. You will be all alone and then you will repent for all the things that you have done and pray for your loneliness to end. But it will be too late, Karun. It will be too late and you will have to live with your misery. I hope you open your eyes soon and wake up before that.'

I sit there in silence and look at her.

'Do you have anything more to say?' I ask her flatly.

'No,' she says as she pushes her chair back, gets up and leaves.

Huh! Girls! They just can't handle another girl in their boyfriend's life, even if they are simple plain friends. Anyway, I am not her boyfriend anymore; I am her *ex*-boyfriend now. And I am not going to regret anything. *She* is going to repent, she is going to rue this day when she reads about me and my books in the newspapers after I become famous. But then it will be too late for her. *Too late*.

41

**While taking printouts of their manuscript
they realize they did it twenty-six times (as it is an
easy number to remember)—Jeet**

And the first draft of our manuscript is complete. It feels like
a great achievement. I have never completed anything this big
before. It's an awesome feeling! We are in Chandigarh's Sector
22 market, taking printouts. It's a busy internet café. There
is quite a bustle as many students are busy working on their
computers, going through files in their hands and making
corrections in their documents. The students seem to be
from many different countries and races. I can see Bhutanese,
Africans as well as several white students in the crowd. It's like
the whole world has come to celebrate the completion of our
manuscript. Most seem like they have not slept in days. They
have large coffee mugs by their sides and look shabby. Just
like us. It's been two days since I took a shower. But I couldn't
help it; it was the last bit of writing and we *had* to complete
the first draft by today morning come what may. After the

event here in Chandigarh in the evening, we both will head back to Delhi and get back to our irritatingly mundane lives. Neeti's one-month fantasy trip is over and my month-long promotional tour is done.

I am standing by the printer to see if the prints are coming out fine and Neeti is sitting in front of a computer to check if anything goes wrong.

The last page of the manuscript rolls out and it's a total of 220 pages. I pick the printouts and set them in a neat, regular pile. I look at the cover page that says *Crazy, Angry, Hot Love*. The title is a total of nineteen characters and that is what guarantees its success. I do believe in numerology—call me superstitious. I flip through the pages till the last page that says THE END. It is extremely fulfilling to hold the printout of your manuscript. It's almost as fulfilling as scx.

Neeti looks at the bundle of papers in my hands and asks, 'Done?'

'Done!' I smile.

'Super!' she gets up from the chair and comes to me as I hand her the fresh laser prints of our manuscript.

'So we finally did it,' she says looking at the manuscript and opens her arms for a hug. I hug her. She smells of days of sweat but for some reason even that smells sweet right now. I kiss her gently on side of her neck that is sticky with sweat and say, 'Thank you.'

After a few seconds as I push myself back, she looks at me and asks, 'What for?'

For giving me my next novel. For giving me such a good next novel. But I can't tell her that.

'For what?' she asks again.

'Nothing, just felt like saying so.'

She turns her eyes to the manuscript again and flips to the last chapter. 'It's funny,' she says, 'we have made out exactly the number of times as the chapters in our novel.'

'You kept a track of the number of times?'

'Twenty-six is an easy number to remember,' she gives a naughty smile.

'Maybe, this is cosmic approval of our relationship.'

Wow, I have started talking like a writer, great! I hold her and kiss her on the lips and she kisses me back.

'We should take it to the publishers now.' I say.

'I think we should give it another reading,' she says. 'We need to see how the story reads as a whole.'

'True,' I say. But I also need to figure out which publisher to pitch this book to. After what Karun told me about D.K. Dé, I don't want to give this book to him.

'But we need to plan who all we will approach to publish this book,' I say.

'I thought we were going with Dash Publishers,' she replies.

'I think we can go to someone better with this book.'

'Hmm,' she nods.

I look at her—thinking hard, eyes narrowed, looking at the floor and biting her lower lip. I want to take her in my arms and kiss her again. It has been so much of fun working with her these past weeks.

'So?' I ask

'So?' she looks at me with a questioning frown.

'When do we start working on our next book?'

'Ha ha! This one is not done yet. But yes, we will start the next one soon.'

'So, are we a team?'

'Team.' She smiles.

42

Pain and hurt is only fuel for some—Karun

I am strong. I am not going to let the fact that Lovanya ditched me pull me down in any way. It's her loss, not mine. I am going to harden my heart. And who says I don't have friends? Devika has been so concerned about me since the day Lovanya and I broke up. She has been the only one I can trust these days actually. I called Devika as soon as I came back after meeting Lovanya. I told Devika the lame story about the mail that Lovanya made up. She was quite shocked to hear it. Lovanya has gone mad with jealousy. Devika was not only really sorry to hear what had happened, she also asked if I wanted to go somewhere to make myself feel better. I didn't want to go anywhere but she insisted. She said there's a wonderful place that she always goes to whenever she is upset. So here we are—sitting on top of the water tank on the rooftop of a housing tower. The view is marvellous. The sun is setting and I can literally see the whole of Gurgaon. The orange light of sunset colours the sky and birds are flying to the horizon. Maybe they are heading home. What a fantastic skyline—the tall buildings are silhouetted against the light, the details of their facades are vanishing. Beyond the buildings are the rigid, stony Aravallis. This is the city, the city of power. People live in these expensive houses and own expensive cars. And one day I will be a famous personality here. Everyone will know my name.

I see Devika climbing the ladder to the water tank with two bottles of Coke in her hands.

'It's an amazing place, isn't it? Whenever I am sad, this place never fails to lighten my heart.'

I look at her and smile, 'I wonder how many times your heart has been broken.' The cool breeze lightly ruffles my hair.

'The answer to that would be never. I don't give people the right to break my heart. It belongs to me and I am the one who gets to decide when and how it breaks,' she says, opening her bottle of Coke and taking a sip.

'I wish I had followed that,' I say as I let out a little laugh looking at the hills far away.

'Come on, Karun, be a man, yaar! And you've got to understand Lovanya's point of view too. Not everyone can be with someone who is famous. Such a relationship calls for a deep understanding. And only someone with similar desires can understand that.' We sit in silence for a few seconds looking at the busy evening road that curves and slithers like a snake through the city. The cars and bikes look like toys to play with from this distance.

'But if you ask me, I would suggest you make a rule to always stay away from relationships if you really want to be successful. The people you love only tie you down and keep you away from success. And according to that school of thought you should be happy about your break-up—you are free for success,' she says taking another sip from her bottle.

'Do you really believe that?' I ask.

'With all my heart,' she says dramatically, like a film actress, putting a hand on her chest. 'And believe me, one day you will be thankful that you broke up with Lovanya. I told you before as well, she was not the one for you.'

I look into her eyes as she says this. Was I wrong to choose Lovanya? Is Devika the one for me, I ask myself as she looks right back into my eyes.

She puts her hand on mine and squeezes it gently. 'Don't worry, you will get over it. Everyone does. Devdas does not exist in our world any more, he died long ago,' she says as she turns her head and looks at the sunset.

43

Maybe he is hesitant to make a public appearance because he thinks that he looks like a monkey (…or a horse … or a donkey … or a frog … well, it's hard to say)—Rohit

Hi Rohit,

We formally invite you to the One Day Lit Fest of the Year at the Maddison Hotel.

Tagged by many national newspapers as a 'platform for art and creativity', our association—Books and Things—has been organizing book events by various well-known authors along with local and national music artists, photography and painting exhibitions and have received great feedback for creating an environment for the people, young and old, who love their books. Events like this would do tons of good to a reading culture which is fast developing in the young

generation of today. As requested by our
association patrons, it would be an honour
to have in our presence national bestseller
authors such as yourself. Together with
the participation of literary artists and
the literature lovers, we hope to see a
successful event.

Please find the proposed scheduled for the
event that we are sending as an attachment
with this email.

We look forward to your presence at our
festival.

Best,
Pulkit
0999888765
For One Day Lit Fest of the Year

They are asking me to make a public appearance. They want me
to address people sitting in front of me and speak into the mic.
And it's going to be covered by the media. They will probably
want me to interview with the journalists. Okay, there is no
way on earth I am going to do that. I stare at Pulkit's RSVP
number on the screen. Should I call him right now and let him
know that I will not be able to participate in the One Day
Lit Fest?

'What are you reading, sir-ji?' Pranav comes out of his room.
He has a streak of orange paint smeared on his forehead and
his fingers are all covered in paint—chrome yellow, turquoise,

crimson, black. He has been working on his painting.

'Nothing, just an invitation to an event,' I reply.

'Wow! Where? When?' He is all jumpy and excited as usual.

'I am not going.'

'Sir-ji, you should go. You will get good publicity. It will help your books.'

'There is no way I am ever going to this event, it's going to be covered by the media.'

Pranav comes closer to the computer screen and reads the list of media partners mentioned in the mail.

'Wow, sir-ji! You will be in the newspapers! You will be on the radio! The television!'

'How much of your painting is done, Pranav?' I ask, smiling at him.

'I am working on it,' he says quickly, avoiding eye contact.

'When are you going to finish it?' I ask.

'I am working on it,' he repeats.

I march into his room as he follows me, crying. 'Sir-ji, let's go out to eat, sir-ji, let's go out to eat!'

I enter and see a half-painted canvas lying in the room (which is really, really messy by the way—clothes, papers and things lying all around). There is a new canvas on the easel that has some charcoal lines on it and some splashes of paint. I like the line work. It's crisp and makes your eye move all over the canvas. The colour palette he is using is also smooth and appealing.

'I call it the "Pond of Peace",' he says with pride.

It's an abstract depiction of a pond with lotus flowers and lotus leaves. There are fish swimming in the water and dewdrops on the lotus leaves. Honestly, I am mesmerized by the image. I visualize what it would look like when complete.

'How is it, sir-ji?' he asks.

'Why did you start making a new one? Why did you scrap the old one?' I ask.

'It wasn't coming out well.'

Silence.

'How is this coming out?' he asks.

'It's okay,' I say.

'Sir-ji, you never praise my work.' He whines like a five-year-old.

'That is not what is important right now. What's important is when are you going to complete it!'

~

It's a Sunday afternoon and Pranav and I are out in the market. I seriously don't know what to do with the kid. After breakfast, I got ready and went and told him that I was going to the market and he should work on his painting while I was away. He immediately got up, came running, hugged me and cried. 'I want to go to the market too; I want to go to the market too! I was working all night, I want to go.' So here we are—both of us in the market.

'Sir-ji, have you ever eve-teased a girl.'

By god! 'Shut up,' I say, maintaining my calm.

'Tell me na, sir-ji, please, please, please.'

'No,' I say.

'Never???' he questions

'Never,' I confirm.

'Never even felt like it?'

To be honest, I did want to whistle at a girl once. I was in an auto and she was walking on the road. But I didn't do it. It's a terrible thing. It is an offence. Also, what if she followed me, got me out of the auto and slapped me and created a scene?

'Only once, but I never did it,' I say as if I am denying a crime.

'*Ohoo*, sir-ji, how was she?' he grins, nudging me.

'Shut up,' I say.

'Sir-ji, let's eve-tease a girl.'

'Pranav, I am going to give you a tight slap right here if you don't shut up immediately.'

'It's very easy, sir-ji. There are so many ways. If a girl passes by your side, just hum a song breezily, like Yo Yo Singh's "Angreji Beat" ... or you can give a soft whistle.'

'Pranav!'

'If we get caught, I'll say I did it!' he jumps. Okay now I am tempted. And maybe this is something every guy should do once in life, like every teetotaler secretly tastes vodka once (in college) and every non-smoker takes a drag at least once in a party and breaks into a fit of coughing.

'Okay, sir-ji,' Pranav says, suddenly sounding very serious, 'there is a girl coming. When she crosses us, just whistle softly and that will be it!' He says all this without looking at her, as if he hasn't even seen her coming.

I take a deep breath as the girl walks towards us. She is almost near us as I roll my lips, ready to whistle.

'Bhaiya?' I hear someone call from behind. I let the air in my lungs whoosh out (without any kind of whistle) and turn around.

'How *are* you?'

It's Karun Mukharjee.

'Hey! I am good, how are you?' I am embarrassed as if he has actually caught me harassing a girl.

'Good good, what's up? What you doing here?'

No, he has no idea what I was doing. There is no way he would know. And I must trust god that I am not going red in the face with embarrassment. 'Nothing, I was just out for a little market survey for my books. What are you doing here?' I ask.

'I came here to finalize the date for the launch of my book,' he smiles.

'Oh! Great, congratulations. Where's the launch?'

'The Red Book Store,' he says, pointing to the shop across the road.

'That's a great venue. Cool. It's a very popular bookstore. In fact, that is where I was going to start my market survey.'

'Thank you, bhaiya. And it's on the twenty-fourth of next month. You *have* to come.'

'Sure, I will. How can I not come for your book launch?'

'Thank you so much, bhaiya,' he says. 'I have to go now, see you at the launch!'

'Okay, see you,' I say.

After he leaves, Pranav asks grumpily, 'Who was that?'

'He is a friend of mine. A reader who has written a book,' I say cheerfully.

'He ruined our plan. I don't like him,' he says with irritation as he turns back to look at him.

'You are crazy!'

'What? Didn't you see how fake he was, he had that chaalu look on his face.'

I ignore him as I cross the road and walk into the Red Book Store.

It's a nice cozy bookstore with wooden shelves and lights that look like street lampposts. And right at the centre of the store are three huge piles of my first book. I pick up a copy and go to the cash counter.

'How is this book doing?' I ask.

'Oh, it's doing great!' says the girl behind the counter.

'Okay,' I say and there is a moment of silence.

'Are you the author?' the girl says hopefully.

I cannot escape it, I cannot lie. The book even has an ugly picture of me.

'Yes,' I say, hoping she does not hear me. She jumps up and says, 'Sir, can I *please* take a picture with you!'

She does not wait for my consent and comes and stands next to me, handing her camera phone to her colleague standing next to her behind the counter.

'It's my most favourite book!' she chimes.

'*Sir-ji* ,' Pranav whispers in my ear as he nudges me.

Okay, I can do it. I can get a nice picture clicked. I have been analyzing my face lately. If I drop my jaw a little without parting my lips and smile a little, my facial proportions come closer to the golden facial proportion and I look better.

I take position, configure my face just right, there is a flash, I am blinded and the girl goes back behind the counter. Struggling to get my sight back and blinking like crazy, I turn to Pranav and say in a low voice, 'Pranav, I need to go and meet my publisher right now. He is publishing my books even after I asked him to stop. You go back home and work on your painting. And if you don't work, I am going to come back, chop your hands off and throw them in the dustbin. They are useless anyway.'

~

I ring the bell to my apartment and within seconds Pranav opens the door. I enter my house and see that he has merrily shifted his easel into the living room. I find it outrageous and irritating when someone (anyone!) moves things around in my house. But if this makes him work and finish his painting, it's fine. I go and crash on the couch, rest my head back and close my eyes.

'By the way, sir-ji, I started reading your book. It's good. Whoever says it's only good to be read in the toilet is a wet piece of shit,' Pranav says.

He should not be using such language but I am too weak and tired to preach to him right now.

'Thank you,' I say without opening my eyes.

'It is so good that it should win the Bang Bang Award. Is it a true story, sir-ji?'

'You have never been into books, how come you know about the Bang Bang Award?' I ask, surprised.

'Sir-ji,' he laughs, 'I have been doing my research. Tell na, sir-ji, is it a true story?' he repeats.

I do not say anything. I am too exhausted to reply. After a while he understands that he is not going to get an answer.

'How did the meeting go?' he asks.

'As bad as it could have,' I sigh. It was the worst meeting in the history of all meetings.

'What did he say?'

'I told him that I know the royalty statement he sent me was faulty. He has paid me only for eight impressions and today I saw the twenty-second impression of my book in the market.'

'Then?' he asks eagerly, interrupting me.

'Then we had a heated argument.' I am too tired to get into the details. 'And he said that this is how it is and that is how he is going to pay me. I got angry and said that I want him to stop publishing my book and he said he is never going to do that and I can do whatever I want. I said I would go to court and file a case against him. And to that he said I could go and file two if that pleases me.'

'We should burn his office down,' Pranav says. 'No! Better still, we should plant a bomb and blow it up—BOOM! That would make him suffer losses. That would be so cool!'

'Please get real, Pranav. I am too tired for jokes.'

'Sir-ji, you should go to that event.'

I simply sigh. I don't want to argue.

'Okay, tell me one thing, what would Nisha ma'am have said if you had asked her what you should do?'

I don't know what his obsession with Nisha ma'am is but right now I just don't care. I still miss Nisha like crazy. When I sleep, I sometimes imagine I am hugging her tight and kissing her on the shoulder. Life would have been so much better had she been with me. But I can't do anything about it. She broke up with me and the truth is that I was too dependent on her and was pulling her down. There is no denying that. I open my eyes to see Pranav gaping at me wide-eyed.

'Think, sir-ji, what would ma'am have said?' he says.

44

**It's time for someone to celebrate, it's time for
someone to have an ice cream—Karun**

It's all happening. Finally, everything is falling into place. I am
not really surprised by the fact that my plans are turning into
reality; the only thing that strikes me at times is that I didn't
expect all this to happen so quickly. I hacked Rohit's account
and saw the mail Mr Dé sent him with my own eyes. *He wrote
that he should find a new publisher for himself!* If you really ask
me, Mr Dé's action is quite childish. But what can I say? He
is a psychotic paedophile! I am just bloody seventeen and he
was sending me gay porn links! But that actually only makes
things easier for me. Whenever I need him to do what I want,
all I need to do is talk to him in a way that ensures a hard-on
and that's it. Rohit is out of the game and Jeet is gonna follow
soon. I know he trusts me for what I tell him. And I know
that I have poured so much poison in his ears that he is not
only taking back the publishing rights of his books from Dash

Publishers but will also sue Mr Dé big time. And when all this happens, I will have the last laugh.

I take a sip form the can of Coke standing on the table by my bed and turn on my laptop to check my mail. There is one mail that catches my attention. I click to open it.

Dear Karun,

We got your reference from Mr Dé of Dash Publishers and Distributors. We are really glad to know that you have signed the contract for your debut novel with Dash Publishers and we are delighted to invite you to the One Day Lit Fest of the Year that will be held next month. Please find attached the image of the formal invitation card, a copy of which has been sent to your postal address also.

This event is a great platform for authors and publishers and we are looking forward to your presence at the festival.

Best regards,

The One Day Lit Fest of the Year Team.

I cannot resist a smile as I finish reading the mail. So the time has come. The gates to stardom have opened!

45

And now he also hates his publisher!—Jeet

And the last event for the tour is also over. It has been a really hectic month. You don't realize how tiring everything is till you actually finish everything and relax. But it was a really good month—super promotion for my book and my next book in my hands, it's like two shots with one arrow.

Neeti and I are sitting by Sukhna Lake. It's evening and families, friends and couples are strolling and relaxing. I see young couples wanting to hold hands and then shying away, looking at each other and smiling out of love. The evening glow of the sun casts slow, dancing reflections of gold on the gentle ripples of the lake.

'Can't life be just like this?' Neeti says. 'Can't we always be like this? Sitting by the calming water's edge, peacefully, living a life of beauty and ease.'

'I wish. But one should also be allowed to go to the cities once in a while, to go to discos and restaurants and all,' I laugh.

She smiles and looks at me, 'Can I say something, if you don't mind?'

'Sure,' I say, looking deeply into her eyes.

'Your first book was nice but I think you can do a lot better than that.'

'Really, you think so?'

'Yes, after spending all this time with you, I have realized that some of your thoughts are more beautiful than what you have put in your first book.'

I somehow find what she is saying hard to believe. I would have written something before I met her if I had the talent for it; I had been struggling so hard. Maybe she is just trying to flatter me as she knows how difficult it is to get published and how easily I can get that done for her. These ideas are churning in my head when my phone rings in my pocket. I pull it out and see it's Karun Mukharjee calling.

'Hello!'

'Hello, bhaiya, how are you?'

'I am good. How are you?'

'I am good, bhaiya. How was your event? People are posting great comments about it on your Facebook page. The number of likes has shot up by 300 in the last two hours.'

'That is great to know. The event went great.'

'It had to, bhaiya. You are such a wonderful person and such a great author.'

'Oh come on!'

'You are too humble to ever agree, but that's the truth. I don't know why Mr Dé hates you so much. I think he is mad.'

'Did you meet him again?'

'Yeah, I met him again, day before yesterday. I don't know what his problem is. Each time I meet him he starts singing those songs about you.'

'What was he saying this time?'

'He is totally crazy. He was saying you are very arrogant and a snob and you don't realize that he is the one who made you what you are today. He was saying stupid things like you have your head up in the clouds somewhere and one day you are going to fall flat on your face.'

Bastard!

'But you shouldn't care, bhaiya.'

'I know. What else was he saying?'

'He was also saying that there are some people who write only because they want to sleep around with girls and you are one of them.'

That faggot, that fat fucking bastard faggot!

'Anyway, bhaiya, leave it. Are you coming to the One Day Lit Fest of the Year? I got the invite for it a few days back.'

'Yes, I got the invite too. I will be attending.' If nothing else it would mean publicity.

'That is great, bhaiya, I'll get to see my most favourite author again. Got to go now, bhaiya, catch you later.'

'Sure, bye.'

'Bye, bhaiya.'

I hang up the phone. This is so fucking irritating. This D.K. Dé is so fucking irritating.

'What happened?'

'This bloody publisher of mine! He is an asshole. I am his bestselling author. He has built his whole publishing house on the money he has earned from my book and he fucking goes around telling people that I am arrogant and one day I am going to fall flat on my face. I want to kill that bastard!'

'Calm down.'

'He said,' I say as I shake my head in sheer anger, 'he said that I write only so that I can sleep around with girls. That fucking pig!'

'Well, that's not a complete lie.'

'Neeti, please, I am in no mood for jokes right now,' I shoot.

'Okay, okay chill. It's okay. People talk about you like that when you grow big.'

'But my *publisher*? My *own* publisher? I am going to check this guy out. I am going to teach this asshole a lesson.'

I look at Neeti and she looks back at me. She says nothing.

'I am not giving my next book to him. We will try others. We will try the biggest publisher in India. We will try Polar Bear publishers. No matter what, I am not giving this next book to him. I will finish him. I will ruin this bastard!'

46

And there comes a day in one's life to an action, only to make one's life 'better'—Rohit

I know exactly what Nisha would have said. I can almost hear her in my mind, *Rohit, for once get over your stupid hang-ups in life. Yes, the media should rot in hell for the dirty things they do but face it, who follows ethics these day? You* need *to learn to carve your way through. Maintain your ethics and learn to* use *such tools.*

I have already sent my confirmation to attend the One Day Lit Fest of the Year. Pulkit was delighted to get my reply (or that's what he wrote). Right now, pumping with energy, I am marching towards the *Indian Times* office. I know their paper only publishes semi-nude pictures of actors and celebrities and features only lame stories like Haris Pilton's dog getting a mini cannon to move around in but let's face it, it's the newspaper that sells the most these days.

I push open the glass door and march right to the reception where a cute girl with short hair is sitting.

'May I help you?' she smiles cheerfully.

'I am here to see the editor,' I say confidently.

'I am sorry, the editor is busy at the moment,' she beams at me. She does not understand at all how important it is for me to meet her.

'It's okay, I can wait.' I have to be persistent. How long can it take? One hour, two hours. How long can meetings last anyway?

'Sure,' she chimes.

I go and sit on one of the chairs lined up against the wall.

Okay, this is really boring. I have been sitting here for a full fifteen minutes and can't bear it any more. There is no way I can pass my time any more. There is no activity on Facebook either and my phone battery is also almost exhausted.

I walk up to the reception again and ask her, 'Do you have any idea how long the meeting will last?'

'No, sir,' she shakes her head as she smiles. I am sure she knows the schedule but just won't tell me. How do I get the information out of her? Should I flirt with her to tell me stuff? But how do I flirt? What do I say?

'Nice haircut by the way,' I say with a dashing smile.

'Thank you, sir.' She does not even look at me this time, she does not even smile.

'You look like Priyanka Chopra,' I say flirtatiously.

This time she doesn't say anything at all.

This is not working. I *have* to try something else. 'Okay listen,' I say seriously with total conviction, both my hands on the table. 'I really have to meet her! It's really important and urgent. I have a very hot ... controversial story to give her,' I say as I think of words that might interest her.

'Do you have an appointment, sir?' All right, now she just sounds like robot.

'No, but I—'

She cuts me off, 'Sorry, then I can't really help you.'

Damn! I have to find some other way to meet the editor *right now*.

I look to my side and there is this huge glass wall that gives me a full view of the office. It's bustling with people darting from one cabin to another, just like in the movies. The movies these days are good I tell you, they get all the details right. At the end of the huge hall is a door that reads EDITOR. I need to reach there.

I am sure there is no meeting on. The editor is just chatting on the phone and discussing how her mother-in-law forced her to wear that (ugly) suit again. I take a quick look around— right now there is only one security guard and he is also sitting outside the main door. All I need to do is run to the editor's office as fast as I can so no one can catch me, get inside and scream, '*Is there no justice left in this world? Does no one care about the truth and what is right?* Just like Sunny Deol. This will take her complete by surprise and make her do as I say. It's rather simple I think.

~

Okay, it didn't go as planned. And it turns out that there *was* a meeting on. Also, the editor was not a woman but a man. But I did manage to say what I wanted to. Not as aggressively as Sunny though (I was quite meek actually with all the stammering and everything in a low voice). But I conveyed the idea anyhow. The editor took off his glasses, looked at me silently for a while and then said, 'Please wait outside. I will talk to you when the meeting ends.' So here I am sitting and *waiting* again.

The door to the editor's office opens and many people come out nodding and shaking hands with each other. Just then a man in a grey uniform comes and says, 'Sir is calling you.'

~

I am sitting in front of the editor in his office and I am almost choked. It's only now that I actually notice him. Everything that happened earlier happened in a flash. He is a man in his late forties and is very serious.

I feel really small. The gravity of the whole situation hits me only now. I am actually sitting with the chief editor of the highest-selling English newspaper of our nation (which, by the way, happens to be the seventh largest country in the *whole world*). I can't find my voice. I am just sitting here grinning like a chimp. I want to keep doing that or shrink and vanish.

'So, tell me,' he says, looking all important and powerful.

This is my time! This is the moment.

'My publisher is a cheater. He has been cheating me since my first book was released. He didn't even tell me when he released my second book in the market. I have been invited to the One Day Lit Fest of the Year and I need your help!' I say all this breathlessly in one go.

He looks at me for a while and then asks, 'Would you please tell me your name?'

'My name is Rohit Sehdev. I am a novelist. My first book is called *Those Things in Everybody's Life, Big and Small*, and the second one is *Like Those Things in the Movies*.'

'Mr Rohit, please calm down first,' he says.

I nod.

He picks up the telephone by his side, punches a number and speaks into it, 'Please send in a glass of water.'

47

They do not want to part, and maybe they have realized it—Jeet

So here we are. Our grand trip has finally come to an end. We are at the New Delhi Railway Station. It was so much fun and, frankly speaking, I am feeling kind of bad that the trip has ended and Neeti and I have to part. The worst thing of all is that she is getting married.

'So, when is the big wedding?' I ask.

'Ah! The wedding,' she sighs, 'I think I am going to go home and tell my parents that the wedding is off. I don't feel right about this wedding. I neither understand, nor do I know this man they want me to marry.'

'Oh,' I say, trying to sound normal. Yes, *yes*!

'I don't really know how my parents are going to react, but I am going to go ahead with my decision anyway. I might have to move out of my house, I might have to take up a new place, but it's okay. It's better than ruining my whole life over a wrong decision,' she says.

Silence.

'I guess this is it then, this is where we part ways,' I say looking at her. I am surprised at the theatrical tone of my speech.

'God! Cut the drama please! You are saying this as if we are never going to see each other again.'

I look back at her slightly embarrassed.

'Remember the One Day Lit Fest of the Year? We are supposed to go there together and it's not even a week away,' she smiles.

48

The biggest lit fest E-V-E-R!—Rohit

I am not that crazy. I do get bouts of panic and feel that what I am doing is totally insane. Exposing my publisher in front of the public like that has the potential of ruining my writing career forever. But I have to do this. The world needs to know what the reality is—the world needs to know the truth.

And it won't be the end of the world anyway. Worst-case scenario, I will still have my teaching job. And to be honest, I *am* having fun with it, despite saying how irritating it is all the time.

This is not a small event. You can tell that just by looking at the venue—the Madisson Hotel. It is a huge double height hall with a long banner hanging from the ceiling as if marking some royal territory. It has pictures of all the authors. It also has a picture of me looking like a crow (owing to my long nose of course). It's lunch time now and everyone is queuing up at the buffet table. But I am gearing up for the next session. Where the owner of the publishing house that has brought a revolution in the Indian publishing industry is a special guest—Mr D.K. Dé. He is going to talk about 'The new wave in Indian publishing and young authors'. It is during this session that I will unmask him.

'Sir-ji, you are not eating anything?' Pranav suddenly appears in front of me. He holding a plate with more food than I can possibly eat.

'No, not hungry right now,' I say. I am eaten up by anxiety—can't eat anything right now.

He comes closer and whispers in my ear, 'Sir-ji, we don't come to the Madisson every day. You should eat.'

'It's okay. We will come again some time.' If I eat right now, I'll puke. I am already going to create a scene here; don't want to add to it by puking in front of the media.

'... and later the author puked on his table ...' I imagine a tosh news anchor speak into the mic on TV as a snapshot of me throwing up with my mouth wide open flashes at the top left corner of the screen.

The lunch hour is over and people are settling down again. A happy-looking, tall, slim lady with blue eyes appears on the stage and starts speaking into the mic. 'Ladies and gentlemen. May I have your kind attention please? We are going to start with the next session soon. Mr D.K. Dé will be in conversation with award winning journalist and author Kamal Hussain. They will be discussing new emerging trends in the Indian publishing industry. Thank you,' she nods and walks off the stage.

In five minutes they start with the session. Mr D.K. Dé

is sitting in the middle, on his right is author–journalist Mr Kamal Hussain and on his left is the blue-eyed lady.

'Welcome, Mr Dé and Mr Hussain. It's wonderful to have you with us today.'

'Thank you, Svetlana. We have a really fine gathering of young authors and publishers here today. Who knows, the Bang Bang Award may belong to one of these fine youngsters next year.' Mr Hussain says looking at the girl and to Mr Dé and then turning to look at everyone sitting in the audience. When his eyes meet mine, my lips curl into an involuntary smile.

'Mr Dé, you started your publishing house four years back with only one popular title. Today, you have more than a hundred hot-selling titles, of which, twenty-five, yes, I repeat, twenty-five are national bestsellers! Please tell us about your journey from being a one-book publsher to a national phenomena that has left the whole nation, including big international publishers, in awe.'

Just then Pranav comes and sits next to me. He pushes a cardboard carton under his chair.

'What is that?' I ask.

'Nothing, sir-ji. What is that wet piece of shit saying?'

~

The panel discussion has just ended and the house is open for questions from the audience. I am the first to raise my hand and am promptly handed over a mic by a volunteer standing near me.

'Mr Dé, is it true that your authors are not happy with the royalty that you provide them?' I throw my first question right into his face. Everyone in the hall turns around and looks at me. All the journalists are clicking pictures but Mr Dé looks at me and does not even twitch.

'The authors are young and they misunderstand,' he smiles and speaks into the mic.

There is a distinct buzz in the hall now and all eyes are fixed on me.

'Your authors also have evidence, Mr Dé,' I say as I pull out a paper from the file I have lying on the table in front of me. 'I have a copy of Tellson's Book Count India here with me, Mr Dé, and I know an author who writes for your publishing house who can vouch for the fact that he has been paid for only one-fourth of the figure stated in this document. And let's not forget that people who conduct the survey state that these figures are only seventy per cent of the total sales,' I say. There is pin-drop silence in the hall.

'There is no evidence that the figures you are talking about are genuine. I run the publishing house, I direct all the operations there and *I* know the actual sale figures that we have,' Mr Dé says. He is still smiling and talking confidently.

'Ladies and gentleman,' I turn to everyone sitting in the hall, 'my name is Rohit Sehdev and I am the author of *Those Things in Everybody's Life, Big and Small,* published by Dash Publishers. And I state in front of all of you here that the man sitting on that seat cheats his authors of the royalty that he owes them.'

I don't even finish what I am saying and there is an audible gasp in the hall as an endless volley of questions are fired at Mr Dé.

'Mr Dé, would you tell us …' one is saying.

'Mr Dé, please throw some light on the situation and …' says another. They all are jumping on Mr Dé like a pack of savage hyenas attacking their prey.

Just them, out of nowhere—an egg lands *splat* on Mr Dé's forehead. I turn and look at Pranav who has pulled out the carton from under his chair. It is full of eggs and tomatoes. What is wrong with him? This is just not appropriate—not done. The publisher should not be attacked with rotten eggs and tomatoes. But for some reason, I am not angry with what is happening. I am not angry with Pranav.

Nevertheless, I shoot a disapproving look at Pranav.

'What, sir-ji? He deserves this,' he says and throws another egg. His aim is very good. The second egg has also hit Dé on the forehead. I look around and there is total chaos in the room. It's not Pranav alone who is throwing eggs and tomatoes on the stage. There are so many people around. I look at him surprised and he says with a naughty smile, 'I have friends, sir-ji!'

What's happening right now might be downright disgusting and totally wrong but for some reason I am enjoying it. And then, even I can't control my rage any more. I pick up a tomato and chuck it but it almost misses him and grazes his shoulder.

I spot Karun trying to slip out of the hall and move towards the door when a tomato goes flying and hits him at the back of the head. He turns around and a tomato hits him on his cheek. I look at Pranav and he has another tomato ready for him. I look at him angrily and say, '*Pranav.*'

'Sir-ji, I don't like him,' he says as he throws the tomato. 'And my friend just called and confirmed it was he who sent you the hate mails. All five were sent by him.'

I look at him confused.

'I have contacts, sir-ji. That friend of mine is studying computer engineering. No one can hack email accounts better than him.'

That means that there is a possibility that he might have hacked my email account as well but right now that does not enrage me. Right now I am only mad at the fact that it was Karun who was sending me all those hate mails. What a double-faced ... *bastard*. Yes, I know I am using unacceptable language, but some people deserve it.

'Give me an egg, a nice rotten one,' I say as I stretch my hand out.

49

The way to some kinky sex after rotten eggs and tomatoes—Jeet

I look at everything around me and the ideas in my mind become clearer. It's a perfect plan. Two shots with one arrow again. It won't only turn in higher earning for me but also give Dash Publisher a slow and painful death. He should not have done this; Dé should not have bad mouthed me like that. He will taste my wrath now. My book established him as a publisher in the market. And now I will destroy him. I look at Neeti and she is amazed to see what's going on around her. Looking at the eggs and tomatoes flying all around her, she can't control her laughter.

'What's going on?' she laughs.

'I don't know that,' I say firmly, 'but I know one thing. If these jokers can do it, then I can do a much better job. I am going to open my own publishing house.'

'You are going to open your own publishing house?' she jumps.

233

'Yes.'

'That's a great idea!'

'Oh yeah,' I say giving her my sexy smile with my sexy stare.

'Oh yeah?' she gives me back a sexy stare.

'Oh yeah,' I nod, playing on.

Suddenly a tomato whooshes past my ear and she catches it.

'Oh yeah,' she says again, grabbing my jeans and pulling me towards her.

I smile and she smiles back, squeezing the tomato she has just caught into my boxers.

'Good you wear such loose jeans. I have also started to like it this way.' She turns around, walks a few steps, turns around, looks back at me teasingly and then walks towards the washroom.

'Oh yeah!' I say as I follow her to the washroom. My fantasy is finally coming true.

50

As dash, dash happens to Dash Publishers, what happens to him finally? Will things get any better for him … like … ever?—Rohit

It's in every single paper the next morning. Front page news. I headed out to the newsstand as soon as I woke up and bought a copy of every paper there was.

ROTTEN EGGS AND TOMATOES FOR CORRUPT PUBLISHERS, reads the headline in one. Most papers are carrying a picture of me with a mic in my hand and a picture of a flabbergasted Mr Dé with an egg smashed on his face next to it.

The One Day Lit Fest of the Year turned out be the One Day Lit Fest of the Decade and threw quite some light on current publishing trends. The phenomenally successful Dash Publishers seem to have followed no ethics in running their publishing house. Not only did they give their authors only one-tenth of the actual royalty (as one author stated, providing proof), a case of plagiarism was also brought to light—the publisher had rejected a manuscript sent to him as a proposal but passed on the title created by the author to another author who was published later by the publishing house. Apart from many allegations thrown at the owner of the publishing house, it was also said that he forces his authors to put sexual content in their books even when some of those authors are below 18 years of age. The sexual orientation of the owner of the publishing house was also brought to question when it was stated by some of his authors that he only publishes male authors, preferably those who are young and below the age of 25. It was also said that before asking for any kind of proposal on the manuscript, he asks for the author's photograph. There were also rumours that Mr D.K. Dé was involved with one of his younger authors in explicit and regular sex chats but the rumour was not supported by any proof. Later, talking to our correspondent, some authors also complained that the behaviour of the publisher had been so disturbingly unprofessional that it had actually made them want to stop writing. All said and done, the One Day Lit Fest of the Year was not only a good literary event this year but also one of the most entertaining events ever with a climax that almost seemed to be right out of a slapstick comedy from the fifties. And as it was rightly put by Mr Hussain during his session—who knows the prestigious Bang Bang Award may belong to one of the young authors who attended the festival next year—there are so many potential nominees for next year that I am sure it's going to be a crazy ride till the final ceremony. Another thing that became clear after the Fest was the heydays for Dash Publishers has come to an end. The publishing house has now been reduced to not being even the last choice for upcoming authors.'

Hmm … so the media is not that bad after all, they do support the truth (at times).

~

I walk with a spring in my step today. I feel I have won a battle. The whole world knows now, everyone knows the truth. Beyond doubt, my publisher has thrown me out. But that's okay, I can handle the worst. I can self-publish.

I am in college looking forward to a brand new day. I go and settle in my cabin, put my bag on the table when the caretaker appears in front of me.

'Dean Sir is calling you,' he says.

I wonder why Jabba wants to see me today. Everything is going fine, the kids are working well. They are producing *good* art now with deep expressions and philosophies—the kind our society needs to evolve and flourish. He can't possibly complain about anything on that front. Maybe he wants to apologize about the mean things he had said the other day. Yeah! Maybe he wants to apologize.

I push the door open and see him sitting, like always. He is not reading any (dirty) book today. He has a serious look on his face and is sitting, his fingers interlocked. 'Please come, Rohit, have a seat.' He makes me a tad uncomfortable by the way he speaks.

I sit and smile.

'Rohit, I am really sorry to say but I am not happy with the performance of the students of your class,' he says it straight.

I gulp.

'They were producing much better work last year. This year their work is shit, its *shit*,' he says. Silence.

'I have tried my best, sir.'

Silence.

'And honestly, I don't think the work is that bad, sir.'

'I have seen the work myself, Rohit. And it's shit, it's *shit*,' he reiterates.

'Your efforts are not working,' he stares at me.

Silence.

There is no use in arguing with him. He is never going to agree that the kids *are* producing good work in my class. Way better than what they were producing last year.

He keeps staring at me with his eyes fixed. I finally say what he wants me to say. He has been pushing me to say this for weeks now, 'In that case sir, I resign.'

51

They say Jesus said the end justifies the means. Victory is victory and a reason to be super happy—Karun

The sun is setting. And it's time to celebrate. We are sitting on the water tank on top of Devika's housing society's tower and having our little party. I take a bite of the pizza slice I have in my hand, raise the glass of Coke in my other hand and say, 'Cheers to our victory.' I take a sip of Coke and look at today's newspaper lying in front of me. Rohit created such a scene. Things turned out way better than I had planned. After what has happened at this event, no publisher is going to sign him. One horse out of the game and another will follow soon. Jeet has a huge ego. There is no way he will stick with Mr Dé after the things I have told him.

'Cheers,' says Devika, sitting next to me.

I love spending the evenings on the rooftop here, I love looking at the sunset. It's a moving sight, always. And most of all today—it marks the end of Rohit's career as a writer. It's going to be a dark night for him from now on.

The sky is darkening and people are turning the lights on in their houses. Some have realized that darkness has fallen and some are still to realize it.

'Your book launch is approaching. You should start preparing for it.' Devika says.

'Yes, I should. This city is going to see a new star soon,' I say, looking at the vast cityscape in front of me.

52

Seriously, will anything good ever happen to him?—Rohit

Pranav is not home again. I go and look at the painting he had started last week. It's a total defeat—the painting stands there unfinished. I have not felt this defeated in a long time. Jabba was actually right. How can I possibly handle a class of twenty if I can't make *one* kid work? I go to the living room, collapse on the couch, close my eyes and rest my head back.

Just then the door bell rings.

The door is open, and I know it is Pranav. I do not get up. After a few seconds he opens the door and comes inside.

'Sir-ji, come with me,' he says.

I look at him and get a weird feeling. I am not angry, I don't want to scream or shout at him. I am just unhappy that he didn't finish the painting. The final submission is on Monday and there is no way he can finish it now. He is going to fail and they are going to throw him out of the college and it will be my fault. I am sad about it; I am disappointed—with myself.

241

'Pranav, you didn't complete the painting,' I say.

'Sir-ji, we will talk about it later. Abhi please come with me.' He is still excited.

I look at him and am getting irritated now. I am determined to make him realize the importance of work today. I look at him with my gaze fixed and say, 'Come with me.'

'*Sir-ji*,' he groans, slapping his head with both his hands as he follows me unwillingly.

I go and stand in front of the painting in his room.

'Do you see this?' I ask.

'Yes, sir.'

'It's a failed attempt … it's a failure. And it's not your failure, it's mine. As a teacher I have failed to make you work. I was in denial for a very long time,' I pause as I look at him. 'This is not your failure, its mine. And today, I accept it.' I am being totally honest, I look at the painting again. Its incompleteness is symbolic of the incomplete effect my efforts have had on Pranav. Some jagged edges still remain; some untouched portions are still there, uncoloured.

'Sir-ji, nahi, don't say that, *please*.'

'It's not your fault, Pranav, I am responsible for this.'

'Sir-ji, *please*.'

There is silence in the room as I stand there lifeless. I have lost everything—my writing career is totally eclipsed right now, I was kicked out of my job and I also threw the girl I love out of my life, the one who really loved me, the one who cared for me. If only she had been here with me today, I would not have felt this miserable. She would never have let me feel so miserable.

'You are the best teacher, sir-ji, you taught me how to work. Please don't talk like that.'

'I am not your teacher anymore, Pranav. I submitted my resignation today.'

He looks at me perplexed. He does not say anything. Just then there is music from outside. For a second or so I feel it's something in my head, like the background score of a film or something. But I soon realize that it's actual music playing somewhere around. It does not even fit the mood of the situation right now; it cannot be a background score going on in my mind. It's a soft, romantic tune playing on a guitar and I identify it instantly—'Moon River'. I look at him confused as a smile forms on his face. I dash out into the living room and don't believe what I see. It's Nisha sitting by the window playing the guitar. The soft evening light casts a glow on her shoulders and hair. I am so overwhelmed that I don't know how I feel. Just then Pranav comes and nudges me, 'Sir-ji, whistle, whistle.'

I immediately put both my index fingers in my mouth, push my tongue back a little as Pranav had taught me and blow. A whistle comes out, a little louder than the ones I have tried before.

Nisha smiles at me and says, 'Not bad.'

'I have been practicing,' I shrug.

She gets up and we both walk towards each other. I hug her tightly and I say, 'I am sorry, Nisha, I am so sorry. I was such a fool. I was not able to see anything beyond myself. Please don't ever leave me again.'

'I am sorry too. I should have been more sensitive, I am sorry.' She hugs me back.

I stand there and I want this moment to last forever. I feel so secure and peaceful. All my anxieties and worries have vanished. It's like I have got my whole world back.

Just then Pranav fakes a cough and looks away as I turn around. Okay, tender, private moments to be saved for later, when no one's around.

'He taught me how to play the guitar,' Nisha whispers in my ear.

Oh god! That was the reason! That's why he went missing every evening! Oh no! I am … happily surprised!

'Come here,' I say.

I give him a hug and pat him on his back. 'Thank you,' I say. 'And this is for not completing the painting,' I add as I slap him on his face.

'Sir-ji,' he says, stepping back and putting his hand on his cheek.

This is what he was trying to do all this time. He was trying to bring us back together. That's why he taught me how to whistle.

~

I'm lying on my bed with one arm around Nisha. Things are peaceful but there is something unsettling still. It won't be right, he should not be allowed to do that—Jabba should not throw Pranav out of college. He had a great concept for a beautiful painting. And he would have completed it had he not gone to teach Nisha how to play the guitar. Somehow, I feel even more responsible for his failure. He has the capability. It's just that he doesn't prioritize work. But he is a nice person at heart. People who don't believe that work is worship are not *bad* people whom we should hate. They just have different beliefs. The more I think about it now, the more certain I get. I get up from the bed, open my almirah, take out my colours and paint brushes—I want to complete his painting.

~

It's a brand new morning and a brand new day. I am in the living room having breakfast, reading the newspaper.

'Sir-ji,' Pranav calls as I see him standing in front of me. He has a new glow and a smile on his face. 'Thank you,' he says.

'You are welcome,' I smile.

'You are the best teacher ever, sir-ji,' he says.

'I am not your teacher, sir-ji.'

'Once a teacher always a teacher, sir-ji,' he gives me a broad smile.

'What's for breakfast today?' he asks, scratching his head.

'Whatever you wish for, the kitchen is all yours.' I smile.

He stamps his foot and goes into the kitchen.

'Good morning,' Nisha walks out of my room, tying her hair back in a bun.

'Morning,' I smile.

She comes, sits next to me, kisses me on my cheek and starts reading the paper with me. Just then I get a mail alert on my phone. I go to my inbox and check my mail.

Life has a funny way of playing with you and turning things around without warning. One day happens to be the most depressing day of your life and the very next day becomes the best day of your life ever. It's a mail from the chief editor of Big Publisher X. I can't believe my eyes as I read it.

I look outside the window feeling a fresh new start. Birds are chirping in the balcony and butterflies are fluttering joyfully from one flower to another.

'What happened?' Nisha asks.

'It was a query from the chief editor of Big Publisher X. They want to know whether I am up for writing a novel for them,' I say.

'That is super!' she says excited.

'I know,' I say as I kiss her on the forehead.

'But do you have a story?' she asks as Pranav comes and sits on the chair with his breakfast.

'I am thinking of trying something different,' I smile. 'I am thinking of writing an allegorical novel this time. In which there is a fat king, who rules a kingdom in total dictatorship. All his subjects must follow one profession and one profession only—artists who paint his portraits should only paint portraits and so should his sons and daughters. And whosoever talks of bringing about change is beheaded.'

'Sounds interesting, sir-ji. What will be the name of the king? Jabba the Hutt?' Pranav says with his mouth full of breakfast.

We all laugh.

Acknowledgements

Time to thank, again.

So, another book comes to an end. But this time it is an instalment of a story that will continue in my next book. The list of people who inspired me to write this story is so long that it may run into several pages, so here I am going to limit myself only to those without whose support this work would have never come into existence (and who would shoot me in the eye if I do not mention their name in my book).

This vote of gratitude has to start with huge thanks to my parents, my sister and my family. Without their help and unconditional support, I would have never been able to do what thrills me the most.

Vaishali Mathur, my wonderful editor—it has been so much fun working with you. I had never worked with such a dedicated editor before. You are the most honest and genuine editor I have ever met. Thank you so much for bringing this book to life and believing in this story. And thank you for being so patient with me. I know it's not easy to sit through my jumping phone calls when I get new ideas. ☺

Bhaskar Bhatt—no matter what I say or do, I will never be able to thank you enough. You have been my biggest support (and I mean it most sincerely) right from the beginning of my writing career and I can't imagine achieving what I have achieved today without you.

Rahul Dixit—thank you so much for believing in my work and extending the first hand from Penguin India. The first step is always the most important step.

Amrita Talwar—thank you so much for all your support and your super-exciting marketing ideas. It has been wonderful working with you.

Shatarupa—thank you so much for making me read the final manuscript before it was to hit the press. I like people even more when they make me work harder.

A big, titanic thanks to everyone at Penguin India.

Aksha and Guneet—thank you so much for being around and for listening to my sob stories whenever things seemed not to be going the right way.

Shilpa, Shweta and Kunal—not everyone has the patience to read everything I write but you guys have been the exceptions. Thank you so much for reading all the drafts of this story and sending in your valuable feedback.

Pavol—thank you for reading the initial draft of the book and filling me with confidence about my work all the time. I think I have learned the lesson now. It was super to have you around when great things were happening. And thank you for all the pictures in which my face does not look distorted or molten.

Novoneel—thank you for patiently listening to my stories and helping me with your suggestions. You have been a constant source of ideas for me for a long time now.

Narinder Ma'am—thank you for all your support and encouragement and for helping me take enough days off from work so I could complete this book. You have changed the whole idea I had of what a 'boss' is like. I am going to have a real tough time writing about an evil boss next time!

Varun—at times what matters the most is knowing that you have people whom you can depend no matter what. Thank you.

Ayodh—you have been a huge inspiration and a source of learning for me for over a decade now. Thank you.

Ram and Naresh—it was such fun spending time with you during those work trips. Thank you so much for your support and encouragement.

Thanks to all my favourite students: Akash, Shaheen, Nirbhay, Manu, Jaspreet (you were right—I did write a part of the story for the reason you mentioned. And I have a feeling that you are going to love what will follow in this story.), Asma, Shagun, Fahma, Rupal, Arush, Vikas, Mohit, Ankit, Jassi, Gurjeet, and Naresh. It was super fun to have all of you around. And I am really sorry if I have missed out any names—it's four in the morning and I have not slept for two nights in a row after that trekking trip I went on with some of you.

Anuja—thank you for being my constant reader since the

days when my work was not even published. I hope you enjoy this book as much too.

And most importantly, thank you to all those who have read my books—you are my greatest motivation. It's because of you that I write.